A LINE IN THE SAND

A LINE IN THE SAND

(Um risco na areia)

Manuel Tiago
(Álvaro Cunhal)

Translated and with a foreword by
Eric A. Gordon

INTERNATIONAL PUBLISHERS, New York

Copyright © Editorial «Avante!», 2022

First English language edition, 2022 by International
Publishers Co., Inc. / New York
by special arrangement with Editorial Avante!

Translated from the Portuguese by Eric A. Gordon © 2022
Foreword by Eric A. Gordon © 2022

Printed in the United States of America
All rights reserved

CIP data available from the Library of Congress

ISBN-10: 0-7178-0032-6   ISBN-13: 978-0-7178-0032-2
Typeset by Amnet Systems, Chennai, India

Table of Contents

Foreword vii

A Line in the Sand 1
About the Author 103
About the Translator 105
Questions to Ponder and Discuss 107

Foreword

Eric A. Gordon

The novel you are about to read is entirely based on the factual events of September 28, 1974, and the leadup to it. The President of the Republic, General António de Spínola, attempted to assume personal power over the emergent Portuguese democracy following the overthrow of fascism just the previous April. Of course he was not acting alone in calling for masses of people to flood Lisbon, the capital city, on September 28 from all over the country (free transportation provided by the government!) with the demand to end parliamentary democracy and hand over extraordinary powers to a single military officer and put an end to "communism" and "anarchy." Behind him were the same powerful forces in politics, industry, agriculture, business, the financial sector, the media, and sectors tied to the colonial economy that had backed the fascist state for almost fifty years.

Relatively few writers have lived exclusively off the income from their novels and stories. Many have held "day jobs" and still miraculously managed to turn out the great works for which they are remembered. The author of this novel, who served as a Minister Without Portfolio in the post-fascist, democratic government that was in place in September 1974, was a witness and active participant in the events fictionally recounted here. That in itself is not so unusual: Lots of authors have used their personal lives and experiences as the foundation for their fictional work.

What is extraordinary about this novel, and its author, is that he also wrote extensively, as a historian and scholar, with ample footnotes, bibliographical references, and quotes from numerous sources, about these same events. Although the present International Publishers project is to publish all nine books of Álvaro Cunhal's fiction (using the pen name of Manuel Tiago)—in eight volumes, our having combined two—in pure quantity alone, his non-fiction works of political theory and history are actually far more voluminous.

Two books by Cunhal that focus, at least in part, on the events of September 28, 1974, are *A revolução portuguesa: o passado e o futuro* (The Portuguese Revolution: Past and Future) and *A verdade e a mentira na revolução de abril* (Truth and Lies in the April Revolution). Those who can read Portuguese will find in these meticulous studies a wealth of details about this history. (And if I can put a plug in for the Portuguese language, I believe any educated reader of Spanish would be able to derive a great deal—maybe not every word—from perusing these texts if they have the interest and a little patience.)

I especially recommend the treatment of September 28 in the second of these books, Part II, in a section called "Brief History of the Counter-Revolutionary Coups." This 26-page section is itself divided into nine subchapters, whose titles I will give here: 1) The "Silent Majority," 2) The Plan and Development, 3) The PCP [Portuguese Communist Party] Warns and Prepares; The People Fight Back, 4) The Ultimatum, 5) The People Defeat the Coup, 6) Attempts to Salvage Spínola, 7) Spínola in the Hour of Defeat, 8) PPD [Partido Popular Democrático] and CDS [Centro Democrático e Social] Complicity, and 9) Soares on September 28.

These subchapters illuminate the backgrounds of many of the forces and individuals who appear, even if unnamed as such, in the novel.

For our North American readers in particular, I call attention to the last of these subchapters, the role of the Socialist Party leader Mário Soares. With his own party divided, but mostly removed from the battlefield—where was Soares on that fateful day? Soares had flown to Washington, D.C., to confer with President Richard Nixon's and now Gerald Ford's Secretary of State Henry Kissinger, architect of the coup in Chile exactly one year earlier! Clearly Soares was a "Socialist" in the pathetic, craven mold of the Socialist International, offering his loyal services to NATO and international capital.

The fact is, sad but true, that the Communist Party strategy to block roads and railways all over Portugal to prevent a mass mobilization for the coup in Lisbon was embraced by a number of key unions but by no other political party in the country. The PCP, with its almost half-century of struggle in clandestinity against fascism, and now finally as an openly recognized political party, was the only party to articulate and put into motion an effective plan to save democracy in those fateful days. Happily, it had earned the general public's widespread trust over the span of all those years, and they accepted the party's leading role.

It's hardly any wonder that the Portuguese nation as a whole feels a profound sense of gratitude to the PCP and to its longtime leader Álvaro Cunhal for its survival as a democracy.

Factually based as the novel is, it is in the end a work of fiction with invented characters, events and situations—and no, it does not appear, at least not obviously, that the author inserted himself into the action. Cunhal clearly recognized the defeat of the counter-revolutionary coup of September 28, 1974, as a pivotal moment in Portugal's national epic and wanted as wide a readership as possible, apart from his historical writings, to grasp its significance in a readily accessible form. This novel, accessible, readable, without literary pretension, is the result.

Readers will pick up a number of references to the plotters of the coup colluding with neighboring Spain. Don't forget, Spain was still under Generalísimo Francisco Franco in 1974. His regime would end the following year with his death.

I am forever grateful to those dear friends, colleagues and comrades who read the manuscript of this book and offered their honest, helpful suggestions: Bill Gregory, Francisco Melo, Gary Bono, Janice Rothstein, John Mueter, José Oliveira and Rich Eisbrouch.

A LINE IN THE SAND

The old warehouse attached to the little residence now served as the reception room of the *Centro de Trabalho*—the Party Center—of Santa Efigénia Parish. That September day, just after noon, hundreds of comrades were getting ready for a demonstration.

So many people being there made it hard to move about. In that ample space, with all the excited coming and going, you couldn't avoid bumping into people. Different groups flashed their brightly colored flags and banners as they rehearsed their slogans. Near the outside door laborers were waiting, dressed in their work clothes. Everyone had the anticipatory mood of people ready to step forth.

Some of the young folks were standing stock still, impatient with waiting. A young woman proudly gripped a huge red banner. The young people stood in a compact unit poised to join the demonstration parade.

Among them, one looked out of place, with no flag, no banner, with no image of Lenin or Che Guevara on his shirt, and not even the emblem of the Communist Youth. He wore just a plain white shirt and ordinary pants. Nevertheless, it was clear that the others accepted him as he was. They knew he was from far away, and that by night he wandered the streets watching the passing scene. And, strangely enough, he could predict the rise of dangerous situations and would intervene at the right places at the right times.

Beyond the group, a very young woman, a girl really, meandered through the room, checking in with and helping various clusters of demonstrators.

One of the other young women watched her, smiling. "Isa doesn't want to have anything to do with us. She thinks she's a grown woman already."

"You have a sharp tongue, Berta," someone beside her observed.

"That's what's missing with you, my friend," Berta replied.

From time to time, the door leading from the house into the reception hall opened, and a comrade came out. He assembled various groupings and gave everyone instructions. He was the director and organizer of the march. A singular character of a certain age, with

white hair and a pleasant face, he walked with some difficulty, dragging one leg behind him in grotesque jerky movements. He spoke
with different people and then disappeared back through the door
to the inside.

"David isn't getting better—after getting out of prison and then
that fall that broke his leg and foot," one comrade said.

"It's a shame," another commented, "he was the best of them all."

Alternating with David, a young woman whom everybody knew,
also came out from the inside at a quick, energetic pace, giving
instructions. It was Matilde, a teacher from a school in the old city.
She was the first one to single out the house where they would install
the Party Center.

At the improvised bar, Joaquina, working alone, was deluged
by people asking to be served. Cremilde, her colleague at the bar,
hadn't shown up—and it wasn't only that day. She frequently failed
to show up or arrived late. The comrades noticed, and came to their
own, different conclusions: That she had her own life. That it wasn't
fair to leave all the work to Joaquina. That such lack of discipline
shouldn't be allowed.

On the other hand, it should be said that when she did come and
work at the bar, she was respected and liked. Unlike Joaquina, she
spoke in a calm, quiet voice, and her moves were more deliberate.
But she tended the bar as well and as quickly as her companion.

Joaquina often found herself at loose ends tending to so many
comrades. So whenever anyone cut ahead of the others and tried to
order, she promptly responded in her accent from Alentejo, "First
come, first served, comrade!"

And if they still insisted, she answered, "If you don't want to wait,
then get out of the way."

"That Joaquina is a terror! She's got an answer to everything,"
people said—but not in anger, more out of amusement.

In the midst of such a crush of comrades, a loud voice called
their attention. One group, shouting, "*Viva! Viva!*," tried to start off
the march, unfurling and waving their two big red flags. Then the
speaker summoned their attention. The moment had not yet come.

Out of the group of young people, one voice could be heard. "It's
time we left already." It was Berta.

Two unfamiliar men came in from the street, making their way
through the crowd. They spoke in the familiar terms of fellow Party
members. "Who's in charge of the Center?" they asked.

They crossed through the mass of people, and David led them into
an office where Marco also was waiting. And they left shortly.

Weird. They arrived and left just like that, and no one knew why or for what.

Before long, Marco appeared, upright and serious as always. People opened up his passageway to the packed bar, and he asked for a coffee. Some of the comrades respectfully yielded their place at the counter.

Everyone, of course, wished to ask what those two unknown comrades wanted. "Any news, Marco?" someone asked.

He responded modestly and briefly. "What we have been saying has been confirmed. A flyer is being circulated by the thousands all over the country announcing a march on Lisbon on the 28th by the so-called 'silent majority.'" So it was confirmed that this dangerous development would take place in two weeks' time.

As if oblivious to this news, the crowd started showing signs of impatience.

"What are we still doing here? It's time to step off," Berta repeated loudly, making herself heard throughout the hall.

With everything set, the final signal to march was given. The demonstration headed out to the Ministry of Labor.

Once the signal came, Nelo asked the young man with no insignias, "Are you ready, Zé Manuel?"

The mass that had been standing and waiting up to that point, now shot out like a hurricane, almost in military formation.

Nelo pushed through the others, and when Berta stumbled and fell back a few paces, he turned around. "Berta! Berta! You're always behind."

Always was not true, but it did happen that time.

The marchers of Santa Efigénia paraded proudly through the streets, exalted by what they had succeeded in organizing. They believed they would lend a unique significance and energy to this mass public demonstration. But as they approached, they were surprised to see other organized groups, some with considerably more people, marching toward the same location. When they got there it was an extraordinary shock. Every demonstration from the different parishes, from workplaces, from unions, merged into one great ocean of demonstrators.

"Over a hundred thousand," said the newspapers, with demands from the labor movement and against the reactionaries.

But would these demonstrations lead the right wing to hold off on this new coup they had openly announced?

Chapter 2

Once everyone had left for the demonstration, the hall at the Party Center looked empty. But over in one corner, three comrades on security sat around a table and conversed. Rudolfo, a big strapping fellow, another still dressed in military uniform but without any insignia, and another, younger and handsome, as though out of place between the other two.

It would be an exaggeration to say they conversed, because at that moment the only one talking was the man in military dress.

He explained how he had gone to the war convinced he was going to defend the national interests in the territories belonging to Portugal. He had served on the front lines, engaged in firefights many times, and surely had killed some Africans.

"Were you all right with that, Corporal Santos?" Rudolfo interrupted.

Without responding, the storyteller continued. One day he participated in an action that made him feel ashamed. Even now he still felt disgusted with himself and with the war. They attacked a village, leveling and burning it all, the Portuguese army killing men, women and children at random. At the end of the operation he witnessed the horrible spectacle of Portuguese soldiers, in a group, laughing gaily, and taking photos of themselves with Black heads skewered on their bayonets.

At that point in the narrative Rudolfo rose, headed to the bar and got a beer. Santos discontinued his story, but promised the rest of it for another day.

Just then an excited shouting came from the surrounding streets. It sounded like a serious conflict.

"I'll go see," Matilde offered.

The owner of an old, decrepit building wanted to evict some long-time renters, aged people still paying a very low rent. The owner bellowed and threatened, but met with a firm refusal also in raised voices.

Matilde walked around the neighborhood appealing for help, and a crowd gathered at the building. "No one can throw you out," Matilde said. "As for you," she added, directing herself to the landlord, "you better leave now while you can."

The owner ended up giving in, and the renters continued to live in the ruin of a building.

A bunch of the most enthusiastic ones accompanied Matilde back to the Center.

Marco learned what had happened and went to the bar for a coffee, but left immediately. He had parked the car he was driving at the door. But this time he left the reception hall and stepped directly onto the street.

"Why isn't he taking the car today?" asked a comrade who was not familiar with Marco's habits.

"Don't worry," Joaquina told him. "He's going to buy tobacco."

That was in fact the reason. It had been decided to forbid smoking in the offices, permitted only in the larger reception space, which is where Marco habitually went to smoke. And when he was out of cigarettes he'd go to a convenience store not far away to stock up.

That day he had an unexpected encounter. At the store, also buying tobacco, was a man whose face looked familiar. They left at the same time, and once on the street he approached him.

"Hey, aren't you Marco?"

Many years had passed. They had not seen one another since trade school. "Ah, yes, now I recognize you. Virgolino!" and they shook hands.

So the conversation started, but it ended badly.

His former classmate said he knew Marco had been in prison, but since that time hadn't heard any further news of him. "So what are you doing now?"

"I work," Marco answered.

"And are you still a Communist?" Virgolino asked with an ironic twist.

The conversation soured. Virgolino let loose a string of invective. What were the Communists doing? Riots and disturbances, and they want to impose a dictatorship even worse than Salazar? They want to prevent elections? Organize coups against the constituted powers? And now they want to stop the huge demonstration of support for the president called by legally organized democratic parties who have the total and recognized right to march?

Marco listened calmly. This did not seem like the person or the occasion to get into an argument. "It was nice seeing you, Virgolino, and remembering our time at school, but I'm in a big hurry."

Without saying any more, he returned to the Party Center, leaving his old classmate making futile gestures in the street.

Other comrades also had uncomfortable encounters like this one. The same happened with Nelo some time back, shortly after the 25th of April 1974. By chance he met a former school friend. Nelo had a positive impression about him and told him he was a Communist.

"That's your business. You have the right to be Communist. But you know what? I'm hanging out with the people on the right. They understand the young people better. They pay us well. They give us lunch and dinner. They give us cars when we go out politicking. And on top of that there's lots of gorgeous girls."

Just as Marco did, Nelo cut the conversation short and didn't care to hear more. "You're a piece of shit!" he told him, turning his back on him and continuing on his way.

In the early evening, the relative silence of the empty space was suddenly interrupted when two women entered, asking in loud voices to speak with the party. Marco invited them into the office to see what this was about.

They didn't waste any time before speaking out. The situation in the clothing factory was unbearable. The day before, the factory owner, a Swedish woman, told them that with the disturbances all over, the threat of a civil war, the revolts and the excessive demands and requirements of the workers, conditions did not allow the factory to continue operating.

And that morning, when they arrived at work, they were very upset to see the Swedish lady, supported by a detachment from the police, trying to remove sewing machines and fabric cutters from the factory. At the very moment when all these women workers arrived, some of the machines were already in the street waiting to be carried away in a truck the owner had parked there.

An immediate general and spontaneous resistance broke out. Making a noisy racket, the women en masse surrounded the Swedish woman, the police and the movers, placing themselves prominently at the front.

"She wants to take everything away and close the factory," said one woman.

"And not pay our back wages," another added.

Despite the workers' determination, they didn't know if they had the power to stop the factory owner's plans.

"It's not far. I'll go there with you," said Marco. And passing through the reception hall, he asked Luís, "Do you want to come with me?"

He informed David and left with the women. On the way there he noticed that Isa was following right behind them. "This isn't a matter for you, girl. Don't come and get into this mess."

Isa didn't answer, but continued to follow him and Luís and the two women as part of the group.

As soon as they arrived, the workers, shouting their protests, opened the way for them.

"Go, Glória, go!" said one. "They're still trying to take the machines out."

With their way clear, the Party group headed right into the middle of all the confusion. As they continued to yell and protest, the garment workers surrounded the machines and placed themselves protectively in front of them. The police were there, protecting the Swedish lady. There was some pushing and shoving, but the situation was nowhere near being resolved.

Marco walked directly up to the police. "This isn't your affair. What are you guys doing here?"

"And who are you to talk to us like that?"

"I represent the Communist Party. That's enough."

"And your party, what right does it have to get involved in this?" one policeman replied.

Without answering him, Marco explained himself. This was about a labor conflict, and the police had no business being there. They should let the workers and the boss settle the matter.

The police insisted on the owner's rights, and Marco insisted the police had no reason to be there. "What do you think? That the 25th of April never happened?"

Already standing at the sewing machines, Glória and Rosário, the two workers who had gone to the Party Center, demanded to carry them back into the factory.

"Like it or not, the machines stay in the factory," Glória persisted. "We're gonna take them inside and that's the end of it."

It went on like that all morning. The police slackened up their guard around the owner. And finally, whooping with joy, the workers brought all the machines back inside and triumphantly appeared out on the street again.

The Swedish lady closed the door, and boomed furiously, "You'll see tomorrow. For better or worse."

The workers decided to remain there all night in case the owner tried doing then what she could not do during the day.

Marco stayed with them until late, and only left when it was already dark. He advised them not to leave the site.

"Tomorrow morning, at the start of the work day, I'll be here with you. They couldn't gut the factory yesterday, and they won't tomorrow either."

Shortly after Marco left, Lídice, who was David's companion in underground life, showed up. She usually did, but during these times of imminent danger, more often. Now she worked in Party promotion, bringing posters, stickers, rolls of cloth and newspapers. She left soon after.

"It's sad," said Cremilde, Joaquina's co-worker at the bar.

"Yes, it's sad, but the separation was inevitable," Joaquina agreed, then expanded on the subject. She's young and full of life. He was still a great comrade, a sweet man, but for her he's very old, and the accident, just a few days after he got out of prison, put him in that condition. Dragging his leg like that, he can hardly walk.

They talked about him, and her, but there was one thing they didn't know. Everyone knew they had lived together clandestinely, in one of those houses quickly set up to harbor this or that comrade. But no one knew if the connection between them was merely the result of friendship and the understanding that they were in for a prolonged period of isolation, one that arose spontaneously, as nature would have it, or if they truly loved one another. Or if, when they separated, after the 25th of April, there had been some serious disagreement that led them to part. No one knew the real story except for them, and they kept it to themselves.

That's why it was hard to know if the glance Lídice cast in the direction of the door leading to the offices was one of hope or fear that David might appear and that they'd meet.

But life at the Party Center of Santa Efigénia Parish went on that day, like the others during that time, with the hallucinatory density and speed of events.

That morning, too, another group of workers came looking for the Party.

Dragging his foot with his arduous gait, David came out to the hall and brought them back into his office. They sat down and introduced themselves.

"We're from Metalex," said the youngest one. "I'm Paulo. This is Vítor and he's Martins. We represent the Workers Committee."

Metalex was a big factory at the far edge of the parish. The workers there could not remain with their arms folded, protesting and getting no result. The government wasn't doing anything. And COPCON[1] wasn't doing anything either to settle the situation.

---

1. COPCON was the Comando Operacional do Continente—the Continental Operational Command—a political-military command for Portugal created by the Armed Forces Movement in the period following the 25th of April 1974 Revolution. It was dissolved after the coup of the 25th of November 1975.

"They think it's an open field and they're destroying the factory."
They were canceling orders, stopping work in some departments,
firing employees, illegally withdrawing monies and sending them to
Switzerland or depositing them in the name of some straw men. In
the end, they're ruining the business and sabotaging the economy. It
was necessary for the Party to put pressure on the government they
were part of, and on COPCON, for them to intervene and resolve
the situation.

David pointed out that this kind of sabotage was part of the
buildup toward the gigantic demonstration of the "silent majority."

It was known that the big bankers and industrialists were financ-
ing the preparations for the coup. They had even formed and
publicized a group with the participation of the biggest capitalists
who promised—should the coup succeed, the government fall,
COPCON be liquidated and the Communists kicked out—to invest
120 million *contos* and guarantee the creation of 150,000 more jobs.
"What's happening in your factory has to be seen in the light of the
present situation," he explained.

"Our workers are resisting and they're ready to fight. But con-
cretely, what do we do?" Paulo asked.

David answered quickly and without hesitation. "Occupy the
factory and keep it running." And when he saw the incredulous
expression on Martins's face, he underscored it again. "Occupy the
factory. And if the owner appears, don't let him in."

The representatives said they had decided to hold a plenary meeting of the workers the following morning, at the start of the workday.

"Comrade Gabriel will be with you there tomorrow to help. You
may not know him, but he's part of the leadership of the parish
organization."

"Have him look for one of us," Paulo ended.

At lunchtime that same day an unexpected visitor came to the
Center, a man of respectable appearance who had been seen around
the parish, with a serious, stiff air about him. All eyes turned toward
him as he entered, tall and erect, impeccably well dressed in a suit
and tie.

"What does this character want here?" asked one of the comrades.

"He must have come here by mistake," said another.

But no, it was no mistake. He asked to speak to the "chief" of the
Center, and David met with him.

What brought him there could be summed up in a few words.
He was a Socialist, but as far as the demonstration on the 28th was
concerned, he didn't understand the silence of his own party, and he

supported the Communist Party in its intense agitation against the coup. He didn't ask for anything or offer anything. He just wanted to come and say that, so that no one would look askance at him.

Having said it, he left just as he had entered, stiff and correct before the amazed comrades.

As soon as they got David's attention at the bar they asked him, "What did that guy want?"

David answered in the briefest possible way. "To unburden his conscience."

"If he has one," Matilde remarked.

"In any case, it's a good sign."

* * *

The Center came alive again when the comrades who had gone to the demonstration returned, most of them young people.

"You can't imagine it, Joaquina, you can't," said Berta as she sat in the bar eating a sandwich. "I never thought there'd be so many people. More than a hundred thousand is what they were saying there." And not satisfied with that, she added, "There were more than that, I'm sure, many more."

Taking advantage of some free time without specific tasks to perform, Nelo, Berta, Mila and Zé Manuel met in their little office to analyze the mood among young people at that exact juncture.

The overall climate and the participation in the parish were both very positive. Many youths who were not Communists from other parishes had gone to the demonstration with the same level of enthusiasm. When the comrades distributing propaganda on the street approached people, the leaflets were received with undeniable gusto.

But in other parts of the city the situation was quite different. Mila offered some sober balance reporting that at her school the mood in the last few months was one of heightened anticommunism. "I'm always getting taunts and insults and threats of aggression. Everyone there is either right-wing or ultra-left, and some show off their party emblems."

Nelo called attention to the need to spread their work beyond the parish, especially their propaganda efforts. "The situation will not be changed in a few days, but things will be much easier if we defeat the president's and the silent majority's coup."

They spent the day, one like many others in recent weeks, full of activity and surprises. Everything would have gone as it had over the last few days if they hadn't noticed one strange and worrisome fact: Gabriel's absence.

Throughout the day many comrades noticed he was missing. Why didn't he march in the demonstration? Where was he? Every day he was there at the Center and all of a sudden, on this action-packed day, no one had heard from him. Was he ill? Did something disastrous happen to him?

At the bar, Joaquina informed David of what had happened that morning. Gabriel slept at the house where he was living after he had left Marco's house. But, contrary to custom, he said nothing to anyone when he left.

"He had other more important assignments," David responded without further elaboration.

The absence was felt all the more because, since its creation, the Party Center of Santa Efigénia Parish had been known as the Marco and Gabriel Center.

And why that designation? Why were those two names so connected?

There were reasons why.

Chapter 3

Gabriel woke up startled. Something strange was going on at the Fort. It was still the dark of night. Interrupting the usual silence, only broken on the hour by the guard alerts, there came the sound, from someplace deep inside, of people moving about.

He lightly tapped his neighbor in the bed alongside his and woke him with a low whisper. "Comrade…listen—"

The comrade awoke, still drowsy, and in one bolt sat up in his bed. "Listen!"

In the other beds in the hall, everyone else was sleeping.

Something not normal was happening. The two of them paid close attention. It sounded like people moving quickly through the building. Once in a while noises could be heard from the corridor leading into the atrium at the main entrance to the fort. Other times the sound seemed to come from above, from the corridor and cells on the next floor up. They knew there were prisoners locked in their cells and others who could move about the corridors. But in the middle of the night? Besides, the footfalls sounded heavier and harder.

They rose from their beds and went to the grated window to peer out toward the central concourse. By contrast to the rustling on the inside, the concourse was completely calm and quiet—but it was a strange calm and a strange silence. They remained at the window, grazed by the cold night breeze, waiting, but not knowing for what.

After a while, they heard murmuring voices from the window of the dormitory next to theirs. They came, certainly, from comrades also surprised by the sounds from inside the fort, who went to their window to see if they could catch a glimpse of what was occurring.

The strange noises stopped for a few moments. Then footsteps echoed through the long corridor, doors opened and shut, and finally, with everyone by now having sat up in their beds, the light went on in the hall, the door opened, and the guards broke in, visibly agitated and with angry faces.

Without a word, they counted the prisoners, left, loudly slammed the door behind them and shut off the light. There was no more rest in the hall. "It had to be some comrade who escaped," one guessed as he lay back down.

"Or someone who killed himself," suggested another.

In the dark now and awake, everyone spoke up with their different interpretation of the events.

"Nothing's happening, comrades," someone shouted irritably. "Let me get some sleep."

The room quieted down and everyone went back to sleep. Except in their corner of the room, where two continued to talk quietly.

As morning dawned, once again Gabriel and his neighbor got up and went to look out the grated window. A shocking view surprised them. At the trenches surrounding the concourse, the National Republican Guards had disappeared and in their place were soldiers in combat dress and gear, some of them parading from one side of the concourse to the other as if on review.

The entire fort was in a state of excited alert. The prisoners were now talking out loud. Some suggested it could have been a coup from the extreme fascist right, which for quite some time already had demanded an end to the farce of liberalization under Marcelo Caetano, successor to António Salazar, and had insisted on more radical repressive measures that would silence the opposition once and for all.

Still, the day passed with otherwise nothing out of the ordinary. The only difference was the substitution of the GNR by soldiers.

That night, an officer in camouflage fatigues, led in by the prison guards, came in to speak with the prisoners. He coursed through the cells and the halls, saying that a military revolt had overthrown the government, but added nothing more than that. Everyone remained just as they had been in their cells and halls. The next day the guards brought them all together on the main concourse.

The day was full of hugging, information, questions and responses and guesses. They stayed there the whole day and then, when they assumed they would be immediately freed, without any explanation the guards led them back to their halls and cells.

Fear and trepidation emerged with the idea that the fascists had reasserted themselves to dominate the situation.

But no. The following morning they gathered once again on the concourse. The military had seized the fascist government. The order had come to free the prisoners. But only those prisoners who had not been tried by the courts were to be freed. The immediate action was, "All freed or none." Even those who had not been tried in court and would be freed took that position: "All or none." And so that day passed, with family members and a great mass of people surrounding the fort and loudly demanding the prisoners' liberty.

As night advanced, they started calling the prisoners one by one. They filled out papers. They handed over the suitcases or bags the prisoners had in their halls or cells, and led them, one by one, to the concourse and across its girth to the exit gate.

There the gate opened, and the gate closed, to the shouting and applause of hundreds of people who had spent the night demanding liberation for the prisoners. Among them, here and there, a sailor.

Each one left on his own. Gabriel was not one of the first, but neither was he among the last.

Like all the others who were set free, Gabriel was hailed with cheers, clapping, and hugs. Advancing through the enormous crowd and slowly opening up his way, not knowing how he'd manage to get back to the city nor where he'd stay, he suddenly found himself in that aimless search right in front of one of his best friends of many years' duration. It was Marco, with his honest, calm manner and his thin face. He had just left not prison but his underground life which, with his wife Cremilde, he had somehow muddled through for a number of years.

"Marco! You!" They shared a long and emotional fraternal embrace.

"Come with me," Marco told him. "I'll take you."

They waited for others who had no transportation. The first to leave after Gabriel was snatched up by his family, who took him away enveloped in embraces and kisses. Next to leave was a big man with a sheepskin jacket and cap who entered the thick of the crowd and wandered back and forth as if disoriented.

Marco approached him. He had no one waiting for him and had no ride. The three of them left together in Marco's car. Along the way, no one spoke as Marco drove. The emotion was too great to start up a conversation.

When they arrived at the Rossio, the square in the center of Lisbon, the guy with the sheepskin jacket asked to be let off. "I can stay here," he said without further explanation. "Thank you, comrades."

"And you, Gabriel, do you have somewhere to go?"

"No—"

"No problem. I'll take you to my house tonight."

As soon as the sheepskin jacket guy left, Gabriel asked if Marco knew anything about Rita, his daughter. At the age of eight, she had been sent to live with her grandmother once he was taken prisoner in 1969. He rarely received news in prison. The grandmother had accused him, with all his political activity, of not having helped his wife, who wound up dying shortly after Rita was born.

"No," Marco said, "I don't know anything. I didn't even know you had a daughter."

Marco took him home, to a miserable house that Marco and Cremilde barely fit into. They had lived there for several years under false names. They got along with the neighbors, including the landlord who lived in the same building. Shortly after the 25th of April, the landlord came looking for them. He now knew they had been there with false names in the underground movement. But they could continue to live there if they wanted, and he would like it if they could maintain, as before, the friendly relations they had enjoyed without knowing who they really were. So they continued.

"Things will get better later," Marco said.

Cremilde, with her quiet low voice, received Gabriel sympathetically, inviting him, despite the late hour, to have a coffee or tea, or a bite to eat. She also apologized that the house was so small.

The conversation, his first connection with the world, went on along those lines. They once had a dog, but in that tiny space, and considering the intense activism of their lives, it wasn't possible to keep him.

After this brief small talk, Marco spoke of the current situation. Much still remained uncertain. It had only been three days since the military coup and the surrender of the fascist government. A true popular uprising had accompanied the military coup, but they had wanted to maintain the secret police, the PIDE. They had wanted to keep the Communists in jail, and didn't want to recognize the Party legally. Everything was still very uncertain.

Under those conditions it was decided that most of the comrades living underground should remain in place as before. And they had chosen some—among them some well-known leaders—to go public right from the beginning and get involved with the current struggles in full light of day. He and his wife were among this group.

The talk for the night ended with that. They fixed up a small couch for him, and Gabriel slept profoundly.

Since that time, up to the stormy September days they were now living in, they always fought side by side, as they had at the gigantic May Day, in the rapid development of the Party organization, in the construction of the Party Center of Santa Efigénia Parish.

Initially, David and Lídice also were close with them. He'd still be with them if it weren't for that stupid fall that split open his leg and foot and sentenced him to a lifetime of barely being able to drag his foot behind him.

It's difficult to measure what those months demanded of the militants in the Party. Marco and Gabriel involved themselves so passionately in the Parish Center that it became known as Marco and Gabriel's Party Center.

So it was nothing less than shocking that on that day of the demonstration, the struggles at the garment factory and at Metalex, Gabriel's absence was noted. He hadn't shown up and no one knew where to find him. They only had David's explanation that he had "more important assignments."

Chapter 4

They went to bed late and got up early. Cremilde explained to Gabriel that that day, as always, Marco had already left the house. She had a cup of coffee to offer him, and a fresh loaf of bread that she had just run out to the street and bought.

Gabriel ate his breakfast, shaved quickly, and ran out in a hurry with one pressing, all-powerful interest, having spent so many years in prison: to see Lisbon free after more than forty years of dictatorship. It was a mighty affirmation of liberty.

He didn't expect what he saw. The streets were full of people constantly demonstrating, hammer and sickle flags unfurled, thousands of windows and balconies decked out with banners, slogans written everywhere, the people ruling the streets, the people with the Party.

He approached a group of comrades. "Where are you going? What's happening?"

The answer came quickly. "We overthrew the dictatorship, but we still don't know where this is all heading." They needed to guarantee a huge popular turnout for May Day. With freedom just gained, the reactionaries already wanted and were conspiring to turn it all back.

It wasn't only a different situation—a peaceful, recognized democracy—and neither was it only taking a deep breath of the liberty they enjoyed and treasured. It was far more than that—a revolution on the street.

The wave of joy, strength and determination was such that the immediate, spontaneous and almost imperative will turned toward uniting with the demonstrators and joining the battles they were waging.

And then another feeling took hold of him, not any less profound and not any less urgent and imperative. But this was of a personal nature, to satisfy his thirst for affection. It was the desire to run and see, hold and kiss his beloved daughter whom he hadn't seen in so many years and of whom he knew nothing. He remembered the child he had left behind and felt an incomparable gladness thinking he would be meeting her already as a young girl. A deep sensation of love and tenderness possessed him.

Grandmother opened the door and looked at him with an air of shock and displeasure.

"Rita?" Gabriel asked.

"She's inside!" she responded, seemingly refusing him entrance.

But from the interior of the house he heard someone running. Peering out from behind Grandmother, the curious face of the girl appeared. Her eyes livened up her delicate face, her blond hair glistened.

"Come in!" Grandmother said finally, though visibly upset.

"My daughter!" He hugged and kissed her and kept staring at her in fascination. Beautiful, beautiful! Beautiful and blonde like her late mother.

The girl showed her complete indifference with a gesture of retreat. She stood up straight and didn't answer, as if she did not know him.

"You can sit down," Grandmother told him. Rita remained standing at her side, serious and reserved, saying nothing.

"Do you still remember me?"

Rita shrugged her shoulders and said "yes," but unconvincingly.

How eagerly awaited, the visit turned out terribly, an awful meeting.

He left in an agitated frame of mind, not knowing what to do. On the one hand there was the dazzling feeling of being with his daughter and the bottomless love he felt for her. On the other hand, there were those tense moments—not just indifference, but coldness and even hostility.

Great confusion stirred in his spirit. On the city streets, the excitement over the successful victory grew into a delirium of freedom.

So much had happened in his life, so much suffering, so many trials. But for the first time he desired not to live.

Two thoughts crossed in his mind: To regain the love of his daughter and to throw himself all in with the struggle, with the Party and with his comrades. An irresistible anguish suffocated him.

Night was falling. As he walked, the tears running down his cheeks hardly surprised him. But neither was he surprised, having throughout his life endured many hard times with calm and discipline, that now he should feel discouraged and without the will to live.

He was so sad, so forlorn when he got back to the house, that when they saw him neither Marco nor Cremilde could bring themselves to ask a single question.

Gabriel would find out later that a similar situation arose with other children, the daughters and sons of imprisoned comrades, separated from their parents for many years and brought up by friends.

In the morning, hurriedly eating something for breakfast, Marco broached some issues of a practical nature. "For the time being you can stay living with us. You'll have to make do with it. Of course, you don't even have a room, just a little corner to sleep in." But he was searching with the comrades for another solution.

And indeed, just a few days later, he told Gabriel he had arranged a place for him to go. "We have a woman, a comrade, who helped us in the underground." Several comrades had stayed with her. Now she was by herself and she agreed to Gabriel's going there.

"That's fine," Gabriel concurred, but inquired no further.

And so he went to Joaquina's house. He didn't like her for the first few days. She was friendly enough, but highly opinionated.

"You'll stay in this room. You can come and go as you wish. When my brother who lives in Alentejo comes here, we'll have to see. I had another brother, but he died in Africa in that cursed war."

In the following days, Marco brought Gabriel to the gigantic demonstration in the street, and to the rally at the May Day Stadium, to public meetings and other demonstrations, to meet with Party leaders, and took him to an extraordinary event, the inauguration of the Party Center of Santa Efigénia Parish.

It was a given that once the Center was up and running, they would remain there as their work—they, and David, to direct the project. The work was transformed almost as soon as it began. David experienced a stupid, though quite serious disaster. He slipped on a staircase, broke a leg and foot, and spent more than a month in the hospital. When he eventually left it, he was almost unable to walk. The doctors couldn't do any more.

Marco and Gabriel remained to lead the Center by themselves, expecting that David would be discharged from the hospital and would join them.

The two of them made martyrs of themselves with work. But the intense political activity did not slow down; rather it gained new vigor in those months until David returned.

It was too much work for two. They looked around, and to the extent possible studied the activity and behavior of each of the activists, and wound up choosing Meyreles.

Right away he declared himself available. He said he was a Party member during the dictatorship years. With his close-cropped scalp and a focused, energetic expression, he stood out for his ever-ready willingness to take on any job. Where tasks existed to be performed, Meyreles was there. He wasn't the only one. Immediately after the 25th of April many thousands of comrades flooded into the Party and into the Party Centers as they started opening up, but it was impossible to get to know them all very well. They worked, they fought the good fight. They showed up, they worked, struggled, didn't create problems—that was their main qualification.

So Meyreles was the one Marco and Gabriel chose to work closely with them until David came back from the hospital. He continued to exhibit his virtues, but also some defects incompatible with his new responsibilities. He was a natural authoritarian, and the power went to his head.

He gave orders, ridiculous orders sometimes, every which way, to everyone, men and women alike, old-timers and new members. "Joaquina, leave the bar for a minute and straighten up the chairs and tables." "Berta, take these newspapers. Read them carefully and bring me your notes on the most important news." "Nelo, go out and buy me some tobacco, a pack of Portuguese Smooths, don't forget."

He interfered with the work and aroused resistance. Joaquina calmly started the revolt.

"You want me to leave the bar and go arrange chairs? Okay. So you come and make the coffee then. And since you don't know how to do it, everything will be spoiled and we'll be in a real mess."

Meyreles found a compromise exit strategy: "All right. Make the coffee and then straighten out the chairs."

The situation could not go on like that.

Nelo was the first to explode. Just as the young comrades were beginning their meeting, Meyreles appeared, as usual. "Nelo, go out and buy me cigarettes."

Nelo pretended not to hear. Meyreles repeated, "Didn't you hear me? Stop talking and go out and buy me my cigarettes."

Nelo blurted out, "Go yourself! And let me work."

In a fury, Meyreles left the little office where the young people met, yelling words that no one understood.

Berta rose to the occasion. "He's making progress. The comrade's now talking in foreign languages."

Comrades who were in the corridor when he left understood perfectly what he was saying: "This isn't a party any more, it's nothing. It's pure anarchy."

When they became apprised of the situation, Marco and Gabriel decided to intervene. "Comrade," Marco said, "we've been looking at your work. It would be best if you took on other tasks. We two, with Matilde, will keep it going until David gets back."

"This is rich!" Meyreles responded, in a foul mood and excitable. "We work ourselves to exhaustion and this is our pay."

Marco explained better. "We are used to collective work and we wish to continue doing that. You know, comrade, leading is not commanding. Distributing tasks is not giving orders, and even worse when they're not appropriate."

Without another word, Meyreles left the office, impetuously slamming the door on his way out. For a long time no one saw him or heard anything about him.

So for some months it was Marco and Gabriel, with Matilde's help, left to direct the Center.

Chapter 5

Now the three of them—Marco, Gabriel and David—with Matilde, were supporting, helping and guiding the struggles of the workers, the youth, and the general population with the experience and wisdom they had gained through the Party. They were working on the parish level, with the broad contacts and ties they had established, to prepare the popular mobilization to cut off at the pass the march of the "silent majority" on Lisbon.

Indefatigably, as the gravity of the situation demanded, they gave themselves over without reservation to Party activity.

Meanwhile, such activity did not obliterate the personal problems that everyone was experiencing so intensely. These minor factors, of which history doesn't speak, testified to the valor and character of people. The fingers of your hands were not enough to count off how many issues arose in the course of a single day.

Despite having returned home very late, these four arrived at the Center early the next morning, well before Joaquina.

They evaluated the activities currently in motion and in particular the struggles of the previous day.

"Things won't get resolved by compromise," said David. "If the bosses continue to sabotage and liquidate their businesses, it's time for the workers to take control of them."

"If conditions permit," both Marco and Gabriel stressed.

"That's what I said to Metalex. If I was wrong, we will correct it."

They divided up their tasks.

Marco would return to the garment factory where the workers had decided to spend the night in front of its doors. Gabriel, as David had promised, would attend the open meeting at Metalex and seek out Paulo of the Workers Committee. David would once again take charge of directing all the Center work until the two comrades returned. And that's what they did.

It was still early morning's half-light when Marco joined the women workers. Glória and Rosário had spent the night there, encouraging their workmates through the fateful night of vigil.

As she had announced, the Swedish woman reappeared with an even larger contingent of police and a corps of bodyguards. A truck with movers also arrived, ready to take the sewing machines and the fabric cutters away.

The workers were not intimidated by this new display of strength and decisiveness. Their protests heightened in tone. Only by brute force did the police and bodyguards succeed in breaking a pathway through the compact mass of workers and arrive finally at the factory door.

"Bastard!" one worker yelled in a voice so penetrating that she could be heard by everyone, even over the deafening noise of the protesters. "You didn't get the machines yesterday, and you won't get them today!"

Protected by a powerful cordon of police, the Swede, with the movers and bodyguards, ultimately entered the factory. The police adjusted their position, crossing over to the doorway, and shortly afterward were seen trying to carry the machines out to the street.

They surely did not expect such a resolute response. With shouting and insults, the workers placed themselves in front of the police, blocking their access to the movers.

"Fascism never again! Fascism never again!!" they chanted in chorus, a cry heard throughout the neighborhood. Hundreds of people ran to the site to support the workers.

"Fascism never again!!"

As he had the previous day, Marco went directly to confront the police. "Who sent you to come here? Not the government, I know. And not COPCON either. So who was it?"

Conversation could hardly take place in the midst of all that racket. With all the protesting, they had to shout to be heard. But what Marco said was heard and gave heart to the resistance.

"It's a labor issue," Marco insisted. "The police have nothing to do with it."

The standoff lasted a very long time. After many hours the police started to show signs of fatigue. They kept pushing back, but gradually more gently. Some of them quietly voiced sympathy for the women. "You're right," one said. "That lady is a real bitch."

"We came because we were ordered to come," another one justified himself. "What would you have us do?"

The whole morning passed, and the Swedish lady did not get the machines out to the street so they could be carried away. The police were getting visibly tired and impatient. One of them initiated the dispersal: "It's lunchtime, and we're not doing anything here," and without skipping a beat he abandoned the site.

Two or three followed him. But among those who stayed, their defense of the attempt to haul the machines out the factory door became ever more feeble. In the end the whole contingent disbanded, except the police officer, who stayed to the end. What could he do, though, but scream and roar like a madman, with the fury of a general who sees, from one moment to the next, he's without any troops. But his screams did not provide the Swedish woman the power needed to bring her plan to fruition.

A great hurrah rose up to greet the police retreat.

The bodyguards were now useless. With difficulty, their ears hurting from the noisy crowd, they snaked their way out through the assembled masses and made their escape.

"Let's put an end to this. And now?" Glória asked. "I see only one solution."

"Now," Marco responded, "let's do what you're thinking. Take control of the factory and continue working."

Somewhat less spontaneous, and more organized, was the workers' plenary at Metalex.

The three hundred workers at the company met outside the factory doors to decide what to do.

Gabriel arrived early, asked for Paulo, and connected with the Workers Committee.

They had erected a small platform for whoever wanted to speak.

Paulo was first to hold forth, in the name of the Workers Committee. He gave a short summary of the situation at the company, of the sabotage the boss was committing, the firings and the unpaid back wages. "We cannot allow things to go on like this," he said. If they did not act decisively, it wouldn't be long before the business was ruined and would end up closing its doors and leaving the whole workforce unemployed.

From one worker near the platform came this shout: "Fine, but what we need to discuss and decide is what to do in this situation."

The worker who followed Paulo on the platform agreed that the situation was as Paulo had described it, and they could not stand by with their arms folded. "But what to do? There's only one way out of this. Declare an immediate strike."

As the applause resounded through the crowd, Paulo and Gabriel exchanged impressions. They shared the same opinion. Paulo expressed it: "Comrades! Many times we've conducted a strike and we achieved quite a few rights for the workers. But that's not the present situation. With a strike, the factory owner, still sitting in his office, remains with his hands free to go on sabotaging the business, denying our rights, dividing the workers and retaliating against us."

The guy supporting the declaration of a strike reacted. "If that's how it is, then it's better to leave things as they are, and see what happens."

Remembering the advice David had given him the day before, and that Gabriel had just confirmed, Paulo spoke again. "Don't leave things be, and don't strike. The answer is to take over the factory and keep it running."

"And if the boss shows up?" asked the man who proposed the strike.

"If the boss shows up, we don't let him in."

He paused briefly. "Agreed?"

An outburst of enthusiasm greeted these words.

The debate had not ended, however. The same guy who had advised to leave things as they were rose once more to the stage. "This is pure adventure, comrades. It seems like we're forgetting that in just a few days Lisbon is going to be invaded by the 'silent majority' and the president will assume all powers. Then we will pay dearly for our adventure."

At this point Gabriel stepped up to the speaker's platform. "Comrades! I don't work in your factory. But I'd like you to know the view of my party, the Communist Party, about what your workmate has just said. We are preparing a response to this attempt at a coup, and we will not allow them to enter Lisbon. We are confident that we will succeed."

This speech earned another round of acclamation.

The following day at the Party Center Gabriel reported that the workers at Metalex had occupied the factory.

The Center was alive with intense activity. Participation in the huge demonstration the day before, as well as the struggles at the garment factory and Metalex, lent new strength, encouragement and confidence.

News constantly came in to the Center of similar things taking place in other factories and businesses.

Unity on the fundamental issues obtained, but differences emerged as to their value.

A curious argument among comrades broke out that day regarding the struggles in progress. "Struggles over demands," said someone, "are fine." There were struggles for demands all over—for higher wages, for social rights, against harassment in the factories, for back wages. Fine. And the occupation of workplaces? Also fine.

But so far as he knew, in all these struggles, demonstrations and mass meetings, they weren't talking about the main thing, that is, the danger of the march on Lisbon, which was only a few days away now.

"The entire workforce in those struggles is defending their rights," another comrade answered. "Undoubtedly that is something different from committing to stop the march into Lisbon." But, he explained, those struggles for demands were so powerful that you could positively say a great number of their participants would also run to the defense of the city.

"We'll see—" another concluded, little convinced.

Chapter 6

As Cremilde approached Marco's office, she heard a strange sound coming from the little Youth Office.

Riveted by the sound, she stood at the office door. Through the crack in the door she saw the light was on. Then it went off, but no one left, and she heard the same strange noises again.

What's happening in there? she asked herself.

A few minutes passed, and then, through the crack in the door, the light inside went on again, remained lit for a few moments and went off. First there was complete silence. Then the door clicked open and Nelo peeked out. As Cremilde retreated back into the director's office, Nelo walked rapidly down the corridor to the bar, where he sat, unruffled, drinking a soda.

Suspicious, Cremilde kept watching. A little afterward, it was Berta's turn. She opened, then shut the door after her and walked down the corridor perfectly naturally.

"What are you doing at this hour?" Cremilde asked, emerging into the corridor.

Berta was well-known for her quick, biting comebacks. "I was just straightening out some materials," she answered pleasantly.

"Ah!" Cremilde exclaimed and returned to her office shaking her head back and forth.

"Berta, my dear Bertinha, where's your common sense?" Joaquina told her when her workmate described the scene.

Returning home with Gabriel, she told him what had happened. "What do you want?" he said. "Young people have the right to their lives."

A markedly different tone came out in those words, one of understanding, forgiving, almost approval. Perhaps he was reminded of his daughter. The conversation on that subject stopped there.

At the house they found Joaquina's brother, who came frequently to visit his sister. He was a man of middle age, thin, on the short side, with a contradictory look about him—uncommonly calm and uncommonly attentive.

"Bad news," he said.

Clearly convinced of the "silent majority" victory in the coming demonstration, the big farmers and latifundists had in the meantime taken measures, entering into open war against the April Revolution. With the connivance of the tax authorities, Franco's fascist henchmen and the GNR, the National Republican Guard, they had removed their cattle to Spain—hundreds of head at a time. They were firing at anyone who opposed them. They were paralyzing work in the agrarian sector and throwing workers out of their jobs. They had set fire to the forests and even the grain fields, accusing the Communists of having done it to provoke repression.

Now it was no longer just sabotage committed by hired thugs. Up to now they had burned crops and rustled cattle from the country estates, but without the latifundists' open blessing.

In recent weeks things had changed. They showed up arrogant, armed, threatening the workers, shooting their guns at will. Evidently they were hoping for a turnabout in the situation.

The news that came in about the conflicts between the government and the generals, and about the situation in the North, made them feel confident of a complete reversal.

For their part, despite the violence and aggression, the workers gained strength and determination day by day. Their struggle carried a heavy price.

In Aldeia Velha when, with support from a unit of the GNR, the farm bosses wanted to take hundreds of head of cattle over to Spain, the workers came out in force, went to the roads and placed themselves in the droves, scattering them with calls in a language that only cattle understand. They set the herds loose and that night prevented them from being transported to Spain.

In Monte Garcia, the big farmers and the GNR opened fire and two workers fell, grounded by the bullets, and died—to general weeping, indignation and intimations of revolt.

"They want violence? We'll give them our response," said one old militant.

The very next day, after the funeral, the workers held big assemblies and decided to start occupying and cultivating abandoned and fallow lands.

After hearing such news, the conversation went silent for a moment. It was almost as though everything had been said, and further talk made no sense.

But no. "There's still one thing I want to know, comrade," said Gabriel. "What are you doing against the march on Lisbon on the

28th that's aiming to hand over all power to the president?" The 28th was just a few days away and it was high time to take measures.

Joaquina's brother answered promptly. "Not to worry."

They knew that in the cities and towns the latifundists were chartering hundreds and hundreds of buses and offering free rides to Lisbon. But people were aware of this and were thinking of not allowing the buses to leave.

In his own village, Casal da Mata, they had held a meeting. Everyone from the whole vicinity came. There they decided to keep watch over the farms and the farmers' movements. The decision was unanimous.

Zé do Vale, who was leading the meeting, asked, "Whoever's ready to go out to the roads and form roadblocks, raise your hand!" Not a single person failed to raise their hand.

"You can be sure. The people there will either stop the buses from leaving or won't let them pass."

It was rumored that a comrade from Évora had come up with an even more radical idea. "If you are not certain of stopping the cars and buses from passing, I will settle things myself. When they're all gathered together, I'll puncture their tires with my knife."

Gabriel made note of all this information and gave his own opinion to the comrade. But rather unlike himself, instead of being excited, lucid and present, his voice seemed spent and sad. Especially when Joaquina brought out cheese and wine to enjoy the family company, at least a little.

There were two good reasons for that. One, naturally, because of the death of two workers from Alentejo that he had just heard about. And the other: That afternoon Grandmother had left a message at the Party Center that Rita had left the house two days before and no one knew where she was.

Chapter 7

Friendly and pretty, the adolescent Isa appeared at the Party Center along with the whirlwind of people who came there seeking help and company. Where she came from, who she was, no one knew. People in the parish knew her by sight, so she must have lived in the area. Everyone soon grew fond of her.

Lively and diligent, and available for any assignment, she helped anywhere she could. She painted banners and posters, went out painting slogans and putting up stickers, helped Joaquina and Cremilde cleaning the Center. And she listened attentively when Marco, Gabriel or David made important announcements to all those present.

"How old are you?" Marco asked her.

"Sixteen."

"A good time to be with us."

But curiously, Isa did not take part in the Communist youth group at the Center. All her activity was with the adults. She went with them to the demonstration, accompanied Marco to the garment factory, did everything with the grownups.

Still so young, she looked the adults straight in the eye with her clear blue focused gaze.

For that reason, some from the youth group—Nelo, Mila and Berta, above all Berta of the snappy repartee—made frequent ironic or teasing comments.

Isa noticed, but paid it no attention. She insisted on acting independently and with the adults.

One time something happened during their usual painting sessions. In one corner of the large reception hall Nelo, Mila and Berta were painting their posters: "Youth stand with April!," "Youth is in the struggle," and others.

On the other side of the space, Isa, by herself, was painting banners for a workers' demonstration: "Fascism never again!" and "They shall not pass!"

Well into the night, with the Center almost empty, Mila, Nelo and Berta finished their work. Isa was still concentrating on hers. Nelo crossed the wide reception room to speak with her. "We're leaving now. Why don't you finish tomorrow? If you want, we can take you."

"No," she said, "you go on." She wanted to finish. They shouldn't worry. Rudolfo was there for security. If she finished very late she'd just stay overnight someplace at the Center.

The youth left. Crouching on the floor, Isa went on with her work, wholly absorbed in it, refining the design and choosing the colors for the lettering. Every once in a while she got up, stepped back and stood a few meters away to study her work. If she was satisfied, she proceeded. If she wasn't, she'd go back and quickly retouch the design, the colors and the letters.

At one point she was standing and examining her work when Rudolfo's unexpected voice close by her gave her a start.

"You are an artist, young lady!" Silently he drew nearer to her, almost touching. "You are truly an artist, no doubt about it!" he repeated.

"Do you think so?" Isa said, once again squatting on the floor and painting.

Rudolfo said something else, but she wasn't listening. When she got up on her feet one more time to look at the finished work, surprise!

It wasn't just the unexpected, rude voice she had heard a few minutes earlier. It was the comrade's hands grasping her shoulders and the voice behind her, next to her ears, with a whiff of alcohol. He spoke grossly, in what he said and with his tone: "You are really beautiful, girl!"

In one brusque move, Isa jumped away. "Are you nuts, or what?"

Rudolfo quickly grabbed her, holding her arms, and kissed her madly.

She kneed him and spat at him angrily. She sprang, and a can of paint went flying through the air, splashing across the floor and covering the comrade from head to toe with a viscous mantle of colored paint.

Rudolfo looked at himself, his shirt, pants, shoes, and the floor in that state and didn't know what to do.

"What are you waiting for?" Isa shouted at him. "Get moving! And clean up the mess you caused."

Stunned, Rudolfo still couldn't move.

Isa had already come back with a pail full of water, a mop and a broom, and started cleaning.

"Why are you waiting? Go on, move it!"

An hour later, it was Rudolfo who finished cleaning the floor, while Isa, in another part of the building, put the final touches on her painting.

"Do you have other clothes?" she asked in a soothing tone.

Yes, he did, and he went to change. "Are you going to complain to the comrades?" he asked nervously.

"Behave yourself," she responded.

"Can I take you home?"

Isa did not answer.

When he arrived in the morning, Marco saw the floor stained with paint color. He summoned Isa. "You have to be more careful with your painting, *amiga*. The floor is all smeared and sticky with paint."

"It can happen," she responded.

Chapter 8

As always, Joaquina got to the Center very early. Before opening the cabinet, she squared what the comrades had eaten and drunk with the money they had left in the little tin box. All was correct, as it always had been. They were all comrades, right? A basis of trust existed amongst them.

The accounts balanced, she put water on the fire to make coffee. A little later Isa appeared. Where she had spent the night was unknown.

In one corner, still sleepy on an old military folding cot, Rudolfo slowly opened his eyes and then closed them again.

The two women set to work. It was a pleasure to see them, Joaquina a mature woman and Isa barely out of childhood, putting everything in order clean and shiny. And done with their work, they stopped a moment to look contentedly on the result.

Workers from the old quarter, comrades or not, commonly came in to the Center on their way to work for a little breakfast or coffee. That day one man on his first visit to the Center saw the order and cleanliness of everything, and observed, "You've got a nice place here. You were lucky."

"Lucky?" Joaquina questioned.

At certain moments, the entirety of a life can pass through the mind with the speed of lightning. That's what happened when Joaquina heard the fellow conclude it was "lucky" that the approval of that building came so promptly from the Armed Forces Movement (MFA).[1] But the "luck" was, after all, the extraordinary collective efforts of many Communist Party members.

In that moment she was there in the bar with that guy and his workmates drinking coffee, and they'd be leaving in a few minutes. But that lightning bolt of memory was the actual story of that Party Center.

---

1. The MFA was an organization of lower-ranking, politically left-leaning officers.

What happened was that just days after the 25th of April, Matilde took herself to the central headquarters installed on a seldom used floor of the Portuguese Legion, occupied militarily by the MFA, which ceded it to the Party.

"I've discovered a good house where we can set up a Party Center in the old city."

David, Marco, Gabriel, Matilde and a few others went to see it. On a narrow street sat a small house in disrepair and alongside it a big old building that, from the outside, would have to have been a storage space or a garage, but was now completely abandoned.

"No way," Marco said at first sight. They were ready to leave the property when David stopped him. It would be better to take a closer look.

"Don't lose this opportunity," said Matilde.

"Let's try and see," Gabriel agreed.

After forcing open the rotted door, they recoiled by instinct, surprised and almost shocked by what they saw. Piles of trash as high as a grown person. Cans of all sizes, boxes and cartons, bottles, packing material, old clothes, a cracked chair, lumber, broken roofing tiles and plaster debris, everything smashed and putrid, giving off a hot, nauseating stink.

And to complete the scene, as one more feature of their first impressions, running and squealing every which way, big Norway rats desperately fleeing the invaders.

David immediately proposed a plan of operation. First, to occupy the building and throw all that revolting garbage out to the street.

"If you guys want to try it, let's try, then," Marco acceded, though reticently.

Said and done.

Dozens of comrades, men and women and youth, turned out and threw themselves into the distasteful work. It was hard and smelly. Some had fits of vomiting. Others covered their noses and mouths with a kerchief.

Those mountains of trash and garbage were all thrown to the street. It was an otherworldly vision. It looked like dozens of trucks had turned the street into a dump. Some of the neighbors objected and protested.

With apologies, the comrades said, but that house was a breeding place for infection, and the City had promised to remove all that junk—which it did after some brief delays—and firetrucks with water tanks and hoses would jet-wash the sidewalk and street.

With all the trash gone, they could now see the layout of the interior—a corridor down the middle, with little divisions on each side, and a little bathroom with a smashed sink and toilet.

At the end of the corridor, passing through another rotted-out door like the other, you'd pass into the enormous attached shed, confirming what might have been a storehouse or garage.

Now the question was to assess the state of the building, with its hollowed-out doorways and holes in the floor. And worse, a long fissure in the roof, whose remnants remained suspended by one huge beam of dubious stability. It seemed extraordinary that the building in such a state of decrepitude was still standing at all, and that it hadn't already fallen into one heap of ruins.

Without any special distinction or exemption, Marco, Gabriel, David and Matilde participated with the others in this whole collective effort.

Meanwhile, in checking out the structure, there was a moment when one person stood out prominently. When they least expected it, they were shocked to see a skinny comrade, with a cap atop the white-hair covering his ears, up on the tile roof. No one even knew how he ever got up there. He was trying to grab hold of the enormous dislocated, rotten beam.

"Careful! Careful!" people shouted from below, as they made space trying to escape the imminent fall. Up high, the comrade, in an unbelievably vigorous exertion, was able to reach the beam and, it being clear that it wouldn't hold up any longer, helped it to crash, with the remains of roofing that it dragged with it, onto the floor below where no one was standing.

He did not totally succeed. He prevented the fall from crushing dozens of comrades, but he did not prevent the beam, with its avalanche of girders, tiles, wood framing and plaster, from hitting a young man who hadn't had time to get away. He was scratched badly, taken to the hospital and admitted.

The blow hit everyone's spirits hard. But as in every great battle, this setback didn't break the enthusiasm, the courage and the rhythm for the work to be done.

This, too, was the last time that David and Lídice, his companion, took on any task together. Even after his leaving the hospital, now disabled, they still lived as companions for a while.

Later, life and work pulled them apart. When he had recovered, as much as he was going to, he would go with Marco and Gabriel to the Party Center of Santa Efigénia.

Bright, bold and full of life, Lídice went to work in the promotional department for the regional Party Centers. Life gradually separated them.

Despite disaster and sadness, the comrades were now at the threshold of achieving something great. With the cleanup and inspection completed, they now discussed the potential for rebuilding.

"The walls are solid," one expert told them. "But it will take you a good number of months and cost you a fortune." In his opinion, it wasn't worth the trouble.

David, Marco, Gabriel and Matilde saw things otherwise.

"We don't have time to lose, nor money to spend," said Marco. But they needed a Center there in the parish and they would build one. The comrades were ready.

They had reason to be so confident. If for the removal of trash and rubble so many comrades had come to help, it was more certain that for the reconstruction many more would come. And not just Party comrades.

It was extraordinary. Where did all those people come from? Masons, carpenters, pipefitters, locksmiths, electricians, all came at the right times for the rebuilding.

New girders and beams arrived, doors, window frames, wood, paint, cement and whitewash. Then running water and electricity.

It was no longer the old ruin of a dwelling, but a modest house, neat and tidy, smelling of fresh paint, ready for a Party Center to open up.

The reconstruction finished, there was no time to breathe. After two days, Joaquina, along with other comrades from the neighborhood, pronounced their judgment: "Without a bar, it won't work."

She would take care of everything. She chose the spot—in the reception area, that is, the big space that was once used for storage or a garage, but now with clean, smooth walls, to the left of the door that led to the offices. She proposed that Cremilde work with her in the bar.

They set to work, with other comrades. Some brought long sheets of formica for the counter, and on the spot the carpenters built strong supports to mount it. They knocked on their friends' doors and ended up with a surprising variety of plates, cups, mugs, saucers, spoons, knives and forks. People from the neighborhood offered coffeemakers and mini-stoves with bottled gas.

They brought butter and cheese, and arranged to pick up breakfast rolls from a local bakery early each morning.

It all happened quickly and efficiently, the great work of a collective.

The only disagreement had to do with drinks. After Joaquina received and arranged the cases of beer, wine and soft drinks, and was ready to provide service, a comrade made an unexpected request.

Joaquina blurted out, "Coca-Cola? No! Drinking that junk only helps the Americans."

The comrade insisted, so Joaquina, patient up to that point, reacted aggressively. "Here we only serve Portuguese soft drinks."

As hard as she worked to get the bar up and running, Joaquina was not done. She still had one thing to do. It was necessary to take care of the comrades who spent their nights there on security duty. But she couldn't leave all the cabinets open.

She came up with a wise solution: a cabinet with the bulk of the edibles and drinks under lock and key. And she would leave out a big cardboard box with sandwiches, and another box with drinks, all tallied. And a little tin box with a price sheet next to it. People could help themselves at will and put their payment in the box. "We're all Communists. No one will fail to pay."

Once the bar was installed and the offerings began, they brought in a few tables, a number of unmatched chairs, cabinets, and two little desks for the managers.

They divided their tasks. Joaquina would handle everything related to the bar itself. Cremilde, Marco's wife, would help her in the early hours and be responsible for tidying up, for the offices, and arranging the tables and chairs.

That was the real history of the Party's *Centro de Trabalho* of Santa Efigénia Parish.

Joaquina did not relate all this to the man who told her the Party had "lucked out" in acquiring such a beautiful building. She merely reacted hearing that word "luck," immediately feeling the contrast between that interpretation and what was the heroic story of the Communist militants, a story they didn't necessarily brag or talk much about, but which gave them much strength and self-confidence.

The bar was already fully functioning when the comrades decided to commemorate its inauguration with a glass of wine served to everyone present.

"All right," Joaquina said, half in jest and half seriously. "But the true date of our inauguration was when the bar served its first cup of coffee."

Everyone laughed at her wit, and she did too.

Still charmed and surprised by the size of the bar, the way it was laid out and its impeccable cleanliness, the visitors finished drinking their coffee and left for work.

Joaquina said goodbye with unusually friendly, almost caressing words. "If you liked our coffee, come by whenever you like. You'll always be welcome."

Chapter 9

The group of workers had barely left when a flood of comrades started streaming in. The Center filled in a few minutes for another day of intense activity with an ever greater number of things to worry about. Hope for intervention by the government or COPCON was vanishing by the hour. For the leaders of the Center, and for just about all the Party members, the only hope, and the central Party line, was mobilizing the people in struggle to oppose the efforts of the "silent majority."

Among the population in the neighborhood, apart from a generalized good feeling for the Party, there was lively questioning alongside ignorance of the extreme gravity of the events in motion, and the idea that everything would remain the same.

In such a situation some encouraging events happened, and others that rattled people's confidence.

That morning Marco himself experienced unexpected moments of disappointment and others of uplift.

The disappointment came when one of the most active comrades up to that point asked to see him with an unpredicted attitude. "It's not working, *amigo*. Count on me for other things. But not for this adventure we're mixing ourselves up with." And he walked out.

That was a bad moment, but others were better.

Only two days had passed since the garment factory occupation by the workers. Glória and Rosário came to the Center to speak with Marco.

"Any news?" he asked anxiously.

"Everything's going well at the factory. What brings me here is something else," Glória answered, unexpectedly emotional.

"What happened? What's going on?" Marco asked, immediately seeing some personal misfortune in his friend's facial expression. But he was mistaken.

Noticing Marco's troubled concern, she answered with a rare and mysterious smile. After a short pause she quickly explained the reason for her visit: "I came to join the Party."

"Great!" Marco exclaimed, surprised and moved. After a silent pause, Marco spoke again. "You can't imagine what I was beginning to think. It gives me great pleasure. You've come at a good time."

"You didn't expect it from me?"

"Not this soon," Marco agreed. "But when I saw how you were acting, you want to know what I thought?" And without waiting for her response, he continued. "Here is a Communist who doesn't know she is one."

Both women laughed .

"You too, Rosário?"

"No, not me," she answered calmly and sure of herself. She said why: that she agreed with the Party and admired the comrades' struggle. But she wanted to feel free, and not be subject to discipline.

Marco tried to explain that in the Party she would continue to be free, to express herself and defend her point of view. The same applies to Glória.

Rosário interrupted him, her voice now more elevated. "I don't want discipline. It might not happen, but then too it could, that the Party decides something and I wanted to do something else, and I do it. I'm with you, but discipline, no."

"No one will force you to join the Party," Marco said with gentle words. "But you can believe that I consider you like a comrade."

The conversation stopped there. The very next day Glória returned to the Center to formalize her membership, and Rosário once again accompanied her.

Signups for membership in the party of workers in struggle were frequent in those days. But for Marco, who night and day directly participated in the garment workers' fight, he sensed that Glória's membership in the Party gave her a stronger stimulus for the battle they were waging.

That thought stayed with him all day long.

That night he received some surprising and unpleasant news. It was David who broached the subject. "Remember that guy with the hat and the white hair covering his ears, the one who grabbed hold of the beam when we were assessing the state of the old building?"

Yes, he remembered. He'd be hard to forget.

Well, now David had just learned that he had behaved badly with the political police before and denounced two comrades.

Marco could not contain himself. "He betrayed us! He was expelled, and now he's going around acting like a hero! It's good that the Party knows."

David thought differently. That man who was unable to resist torture under interrogation, who didn't have the necessary strength to give his own life if need be, was now trying to prove to himself that he was willing to give it in another form to the Party. According to reliable information that David had been given, the man ever since had committed himself to any job, without rest and running every risk.

He worked in building and setting up several Party Centers, and the general opinion held that without him and his fearless work, they would never have been able to open.

Right after finding out about the guy's bad conduct, David saw him working again, this time at the inauguration of another Party Center. One of their leaders told him, "You see that *amigo*? We owe him a lot. He always steps up to the hardest work."

"It's good to have comrades like that," David limited himself to saying.

And now to Marco he asked, "You want to know my opinion?" Without hearing a response, he continued. "That no one should remind him of that terrible moment in his past. And that he be accepted among us without qualification."

From David's mouth a firm response: Except in cases of open treason and passing over to the enemy, it's necessary to encourage rehabilitation and trust. Marco wound up convinced.

From time to time people recalled the feat he had accomplished during the repairs on the Santa Efigénia Center. Of course, not so much in these days, busy as they were in unending tasks and under the immediate threat of a reactionary coup whose defeat was uncertain at best. The present had its risks and bitter hours—but also many gratifying moments.

Facing more toward the future than to the past, Marco, returning home, didn't think about his conversation with David and the lesson he had received, but about Glória's emotional smile as she said, "I came to join the Party."

Chapter 10

The young folks left as a group to distribute leaflets and sell *Avante!* in the streets. Matilde wanted to go with them. That morning would be a project not just of the youth from Santa Efigénia but of youth from many parts of the city. As usual, these upbeat, friendly activists approached people to hand them their flyers and sell them a paper. Save for a few rare exceptions, they were received well, of course with some different points of view. Mila always handed out flyers and sold papers more than anyone else—not just occasionally, but all the time. Which was weird because the others shouted, and she spoke quietly.

"Hey! How do you do it?" Berta asked her with an edge of jealousy.

"I don't do anything," Mila answered.

It's true, she didn't do anything. But what was the shame in being so nice?

They returned to the Center bubbling over with noise and happiness. They were overjoyed seeing the way the people of the city had welcomed their presence on the street.

A clutch of older comrades hung out at the Center every day. One said to another, "I don't know why, but the youth now seem to be better looking."

"It's not that they seem to be. It's because they actually are," said the other.

Among that group of old-timers at the end of the reception hall there was one who, whenever he spoke, always told stories of life in the underground during the dictatorship. He lived or had personal knowledge of some of those stories. The PIDE torturing people, sometimes to the point of killing them. The assassination of leading comrades by gunshot. Prison sentences that ran fifteen, twenty years and more. The death camp at Tarrafal in Cape Verde, where the secretary-general of the Party, Bento Gonçalves, died.

When one of the younger group heard about this storyteller, he walked over to them. "Can I listen too?"

"Have a seat, comrade. You still have much to learn."

At the end of some of the old man's stories, the youth said, "We need to know everything you're saying to better understand what the 25th of April brought us. We'll make the time for it."

"You're right, comrade," the man agreed.

"But now, *amigo*, we have to concentrate our energies on the present struggle, and it's us who are making the revolution," the youth said by way of conclusion. "You just saw what we did distributing handouts and the paper."

For the entire day the youth reveled in the results of their morning efforts. Nelo made a propaganda speech out of the action they'd taken. "You should have seen how they welcomed us today. The people of the city are worried and fearful over the invasion of Lisbon by the 'silent majority.' But they trust that the coup will be defeated."

Activity at the Party Center of Santa Efigénia continued energetically and ceaselessly. Marco and Gabriel redoubled their meetings and contacts with the workers, and Matilde was constantly visiting the old quarter making the situation clear to the people there. They went to the factories, the workshops and stores, and to the housewives. They paid special attention to the workers and young people who came to the Center. They also stayed in contact with the unions to ask about the latest developments.

David, at the Center, spoke with some, argued with others, always stressing the need to mobilize the population.

The whole afternoon the talk was about the success they had enjoyed that morning. All seemed to be going well that day.

At night, things started to take different form.

The war of the posters and graffiti went on apace. In the neighborhood, as all over the city, there were fights, clashes and assaults. Reports came in of more serious events. Groups of provocateurs beat up isolated comrades, the wounded sent to the hospital, one comrade in a coma.

In this generally tense atmosphere Nelo, Mila and Berta, along with some of the other youth, went out one more time, happy and confident, to put up posters on the walls along the long sloping street of the district. Then the unexpected happened.

They had not yet arrived at their chosen destination when a substantial number of unfamiliar youth, waiting for them, crossed in front of them. Standing shoulder to shoulder, they wielded long sticks, forming a compact, clearly organized unit. Suddenly, as if responding to their commander's voice belted out in a guttural imitation of some incomprehensible Oriental language, they fell like madmen on the Communist youth, beating them, yanking their posters from their hands and angrily ripping them up, and kicking over cans of paint and glue.

Given the disproportion of forces, there was nothing they could do other than flee the scene.

They returned to the Center, all of them with visible signs of the assault. Nelo was gushing blood from two long gashes on his head. Mila and Berta had blotches of blood and complained of pains all over the bodies.

"They were definitely MR's," said one youth who had succeeded in escaping the beating.[1]

"With those shouts in Japanese, they're really scary," said another.

But the youth were totally committed. Nelo came out to the reception hall with two big white and bloody bandages over his scalp and head. Berta and Mila and other youths came out with him.

He made a proposal. "Let's wait a little and give time for the provocateurs to put up their posters. But tonight it's our posters that will stay up. Agreed?"

The idea was accepted by unanimous approval. Some sat around the tables, others hung out at the bar to have a beer or soda and talk.

"Nelo, you and Berta and Mila are always taking the initiative in these fights. Do your families know? Do you go home?" someone asked. One by one, they answered.

"Yes, I go," Nelo said. "My old man is a reactionary, always cursing at me, but he's my friend and he's used to it by now."

"They couldn't care less," was Berta's response, with no explanation.

"And you, Mila?"

"My dad's a Communist, so he's okay with me."

Nelo and Berta went back inside.

"Enough with all this serious talk! Let's laugh a little!" said one of the youths. "Who wants to tell some jokes?"

From what they came up with, not all of them were very funny, but even so, they had fun.

"Listen to this one," one boy said, eager to tell his story. "An MR meets another MR. 'Hey, guy, it's been a while since I've seen you. Where have you been?' 'I was taking a specialized course in the United States.' 'And what did you learn?' 'I learned how to beat up a

---

1. MR's is an abbreviation for MRPP, Movimento Reorganizativo do Partido do Proletariado, a small ultra-left pro-Chinese Maoist group composed mainly of college students. Positioning themselves militantly against the Soviet Bloc-oriented Portuguese Communist Party, they effectively served as provocateurs against the April Revolution.

rag doll, I learned a little English, and four words in Japanese.' 'And what do these words mean?' 'That I don't know. It's just to see if they scare the Commies when we go out to rumble with them.'"

"That's no good," another said. "I have a better one. A young Communist calls another young Communist on the telephone who's at the Party Center. 'Hey, man, what are you doing there so late?' 'A lot of us are here telling jokes and getting ready to go out and teach a lesson to the MR's. We're almost about to leave. Wanna come?' 'Wait a little, you bums, I'll run right over.'"

"That one's even worse. It's just politics without any humor at all."

"Mine is better," another chimed in. "The president summons a soldier and gives him his orders.[2] 'Get into civilian clothes. Go to a Communist Party Center, and then come back and tell me what's happening there.' The soldier clicks his heels, salutes, turns around and does as he's instructed. He's away for quite a long time, but he completes his mission and comes back to report. 'So?' the general asks. Standing at attention with impeccable discipline, the soldier answers. 'I saw a bunch of close friends. Boys and girls. I went out with them sticking up posters.' After a brief pause, seeing that the general with his wrinkled face wasn't saying anything, the soldier asked, 'Can I go back?'"

That one brought out a good round of laughs.

"I've got the best one of all," said the boy who had told the first one. "There was this artillery garrison—"

There was no time to tell it. Nelo came back into the hall. "Who wants to go?"

Everyone there—and there were many by now—was ready. In a few moments they rushed out the door. Rudolfo wanted to go with them, and Corporal Santos too.

One comrade who up to now, in the light of the situation, had remained behind at the Center said to another alongside him, "Terrific! Rudolfo's with us and Corporal Santos too. If anything happens at the Center there's only Luís, and what can he do?"

Nevertheless, the group took off, almost running, following poorly lit, deserted streets that still late summer night.

Berta led the group to the spot. The MR's were still there. Some hundred meters ahead, they saw them. They had ripped and torn off the posters and were writing with red paint.

---

2. The reference is to General António de Spínola, the President of the Republic, a reactionary who attempted to rouse the "silent majority" to support the attempted fascist coup and grant him extraordinary powers.

"That's them," Berta confirmed.

"They're a lot for us!" said someone to Rudolfo.

Rudolfo did not appear to have heard. He made them stop a moment. "Let's go slow now, I will take care of things. You follow behind, but stay on the sidewalk close to the walls. Wait till I attack. Don't do anything beforehand. And then you can go after them."

The MR's continued without lending any importance to the group approaching them. When the new arrivals to the scene were only a short distance away, a voice was heard: "What do these jerks want now?"

The question was answered with laughter: "The children are here to clean their diapers!"

That's when Rudolfo jumped. It's hard to explain exactly what happened. And when people heard of it, some wouldn't believe it. Still huddled against the wall, Rudolfo at that moment looked like a giant in size and stature as he burst forth like an armed warrior, sweeping everything before him. A footstool collapsed, bringing two of the MR's down, the cans of red paint went flying through the air, and scraps of ripped posters fluttered through space.

Corporal Santos acquitted himself well too. Taken by surprise and separated one from another, the MR's appeared disoriented, forced into defending themselves in one-on-one combat.

Berta and the comrades picked up the long sticks abandoned on the ground and assailed the enemy furiously, more and more, harder and harder, until it stopped. The youth on both sides remained standing for a moment, almost shocked in their postures as conquerors and conquered. The MR's gave in and ran off.

"They didn't have time to talk Japanese," Berta laughed.

The youngsters pulled down the MR posters and stuck up the few they had brought with them.

Returning to the Center, they were received with a hero's welcome by those who had stayed behind. They were still talking about it when Berta, who had disappeared into the interior of the house, came back with a bundle of posters and a can of paste.

"We can't leave it at that. Don't you think, Nelo? We just brought a very few posters, but I have some more now. They have to go up too. Who wants to go?" she asked.

Rudolfo, shrugging his shoulders, mumbled, "Go there again? They're crazy!" and he moseyed to the bar.

Corporal Santos nervously joined him there. What had happened seemed like mission accomplished to him, case closed.

Luís, who was in charge of security with Rudolfo that night, approached his companion. "Do you mind if I go? If you two wanted to go back to the street, I wouldn't get involved, but in any case I can help the kids out if necessary."

"It's crazy, but go ahead if you want to get into a brawl," Rudolfo responded.

Two old comrades who had stayed behind at the Center to keep things under control couldn't help repeating what on another occasion had been said about Luís. "Rudolfo is staying. What does that weakling think he's going to do there?"

"If those guys are there, they're gonna mess him up more than he's gonna do them."

Luís spoke to the young comrades. "I'll go with you, if you don't mind—but under one condition. If those guys are there, we turn around and come back to the Center."

"Come back?" Berta protested. "Why? Are you afraid?"

"Yes, come back," he said again calmly, without response to the insult. "What happened with Rudolfo cannot be repeated."

They left, as though marching in a demonstration. Nelo had pulled himself together, his head swathed in blood-stained bandages. He tried to take the lead.

The MR's hadn't returned, and the Communist posters remained pasted to the walls.

It was still night, but almost dawn, and Joaquina would be arriving soon. Many had already left for the night, but others were still there.

In fact, Joaquina got there very shortly afterward. As always, she compared the list of sandwiches and drinks against the money placed by the comrades in the little tin box. Out loud, she exclaimed, "What's going on?" She counted again. Up to that point the count had always matched up. Now money was missing. It wasn't much, but it was something nevertheless.

She went to see Marco to tell him what had happened.

"Someone might have made a mistake making change," he said coolly. "Maybe someone forgot. In that whole hullabaloo last night, maybe one of the youths didn't know the rules and had something to eat or drink. Maybe someone didn't have the money."

As Joaquina retreated in a bad mood, he called after her, "Don't mention it to anyone. Let's see if it happens again."

Joaquina remained in an especially ill humor. She attended the comrades who went to the bar with an impatience few had ever seen before. On top of which, that day, as it had happened other times, Cremilde had not come to help her.

Cremilde's truancy was noted and commented upon by the comrades. For some it was because, being by herself, Joaquina took longer to serve them. For others it just didn't seem right that Cremilde, who held a certain responsibility, would fail to appear, or show up late so often. And still others, but just a few, believed she was given special leeway for being Marco's wife.

The truth is that the situation was expectable and allowed, and for good reasons.

It was one of those irremediable tragic family situations—an aunt who was a complete invalid on account of illness, bed-bound and unable to move, communicating by signals that only the family who assisted her could understand, those who bathed and fed her.

Another aunt and her retired husband took care of her. But now of advanced age and sick themselves, they had certain days when they went to the hospital. Cremilde did the shopping and performed the essentials of what was needed to keep her aunt alive. When she got to the house, she cared for her aunt until the other family members returned. Then she went to the Center to help Joaquina at the bar.

With her sweet, composed expression she served the comrades, not reacting to what people ignorant of the reasons for her absences and tardiness were saying.

Joaquina's foul mood changed completely when she heard how the youth had conducted themselves with valor. That alone made for a better atmosphere. She helped by treating their wounds and gathering up the remaining posters. She heard about Rudolfo's exploits, and when he approached the counter, she said to him, almost maternally, "I know, you want a beer. Today I'm on your side. Have two or three! They're on me!"

Chapter 11

More than once during those days, when she arrived at the Center and checked the sandwiches and drinks against the amount of money in the tin box, Joaquina found money missing.

There could be various explanations, as Marco had speculated. That there were comrades on the night staff who didn't know the rules. Or, knowing the rules, who understood that because of their hard assignment, they had the right to eat and drink something. Or that someone had simply forgotten to place their money in the box.

But this time there was no mistaking. It wasn't just some change that disappeared. What was missing was the equivalent of one banknote, exactly one.

For that reason, Joaquina broke her silence and as she left work for the night said, "Don't you guys forget to pay up now."

And she looked at one, and then another, as if from their expression she could discover the culprit.

"Let's continue to keep an eye on it," Marco insisted. "If it's someone's idea of a joke, it will all fall apart in the end. Still," he insisted further, "it's best not to make a big show about it. And once the issue comes into better focus, not to turn it into a scandal. Let's watch, and one of these days we'll know something."

From the start, thinking about this one and that one who worked there, Joaquina's attention involuntarily rested on the comrades who almost always did night security. These were the ones who most often visited the bar during the night, to ward off sleep or out of their appetite for a few beers and some sandwiches. However, it was absurd thinking she could discover the guilty party by their facial expression.

Joaquina observed the comrades, trying to get to know them better, and one day went to Marco to bring up the subject once again.

"I didn't want to say it, but if I don't, I'll explode. There's one comrade who, well, I don't know, but when there's money missing I immediately think of him."

"Who?" Marco asked.

"He doesn't do anything else but drink. He doesn't get drunk, but he's always drinking. You turn around and there he is propped up at the counter. And there he stays, for a long, long time."

She ended by naming her suspect: Rudolfo. And she recalled how he had appeared at the Center.

He had come offering to help with night security, and he stayed. Middle-aged, heavy-set and strong, slow of movement, he accepted the hardest night shifts and went out with the others every time he was asked to help with some job or emergency. In fact, he demonstrated that the night he helped the youth crush the MR's.

Otherwise, he strolled around the Center, sometimes sat in some corner quiet and drowsy, other times going to the bar to drink, standing at the counter.

"If it's not him, I don't know who it could be," Joaquina underscored. "As you know, in things like this I'm not usually mistaken."

"I know," Marco agreed, "I've seen that a number of times."

In the wake of these private conversations, inevitably the two of them carefully watched the conduct of the comrades, and particularly those, one group or another, who stayed doing security at night—aside from Rudolfo, Corporal Santos and Luís. If there might have been some suspicion around the first two, there was no chance of considering Luís, because his behavior lay beyond reproach.

Sometimes the greatest truths reveal themselves in surprising ways.

One day, as night started to fall, Marco went to the bar. He drank a juice and paid. At that point only a collection of coins had been deposited in the tin box. He paid with a banknote, took out his change and left. He crossed the reception room, and right at the exit door he decided to go back and get a sandwich. He took what he wanted from the bar, but when he went to pay, surprise! The banknote that he had put in for his juice just moments before had disappeared, and there weren't a lot more coins.

"What the hell!" he murmured in wonderment.

He looked from one side to another and everything looked normal. The comrades in small groupings were exchanging a few words before parting.

He could not get this mystery out of his head. Was someone hiding on the other side of the counter? Had someone come in through the back door, having slipped through the high, narrow ventilation window in the long reception room?

And suddenly there leapt to his memory something that had escaped him when he went to the bar the first time for the juice. When he stepped away from the counter, a few paces from him someone had quickly passed by him in the other direction. He saw just that one person, he was absolutely sure of it, and that person was Isa.

He left, feeling sorrowful for the suspicion that rose in him as he left the building. *Surely I must be missing something*, he thought.

As he dwelled on this thought, he searched through his memory uselessly, trying to reconstitute that moment. That night he had trouble falling asleep. He saw Isa as always, so gentle, so natural, so eager to help, so available. It wasn't possible! The more he ruminated, however, the more the rapid figure of the girl came to mind, passing him and almost certainly aiming right for the bar as he was leaving. And when he came back there, he didn't see anyone going in the opposite direction.

No, there was no mistake. Absolutely none.

He came to a decision, and took advantage of a moment when Gabriel and David had already left and he was by himself in his office.

He looked for her in the reception area. "Isa, could you come here?" Isa complied.

He asked her to be seated in front of him. Isa did so and looked at him, waiting.

Marco spoke quietly, but firmly and sadly. "Isa, Isa. You're sixteen years old, and you don't want to spoil your life—"

"What's wrong?" the girl interrupted in a rapid, detached tone and looking directly at him.

"No, you don't want this stain on you the rest of your life."

"What are you talking about? What stain?" she demanded, her voice now turned harsh.

Marco hesitated. Was he perhaps committing an unpardonable error? The doubts assailed him anew. He remained silent a moment, almost ashamed.

"I don't understand anything you're saying," Isa declared. "Can I go now?"

"No, stay," he said, now his voice suddenly commanding.

So certain was he that he did not feel the need to refer to the matter in concrete terms.

Isa continued looking at him straight ahead, and kept silent.

"I called you," Marco said, "to tell you it was you. But no one else knows or could know if I don't say anything." He paused. "I didn't call you to judge you, but to say that no one needs to know. Not the Party, not Gabriel or David or Matilde. No one—"

"I don't understand anything," a now nervous Isa interrupted again.

"You're sixteen," Marco stated again. "You're a fine comrade and you don't want to ruin your whole life. Don't do it again and that's it. I want to be able to trust you."

And as she continued to look at him straight-on, sudden tears started running down her face.

Without planning to, Marco asked, "Do you go home?"

Isa nodded yes.

"And when you go there, don't they give you money so you can eat?"

Isa shook her head no.

"What do you eat, then?"

Now she answered. "Whatever I find."

"And where do you sleep?"

"When I don't go home I stay here in one corner or other."

Several minutes passed, Isa in tears, Marco pacing from side to side in his little office, afraid he might break out crying too.

At last he approached her and moved to hand her some money.

"No!" she practically shouted.

"Take it," Marco almost begged her. "I'm not a judge judging you, but a friend who's very fond of you."

She demurred, but with a quick gesture, she accepted it.

"I'm leaving now. Stay here a while. Don't leave yet. I don't want them to see you with your face all wet from tears."

As he passed, he gave her a light touch. "Also, wipe your eyes."

He turned back. "You know something? I don't have children, and I always wanted to have a daughter like you." With that he left.

Chapter 12

Gabriel left for a meeting with the employees at Metalex, which was now under workers' control.

Marco continued to stay current with the garment factory, but no longer had to spend his nights there. That factory was also in the workers' hands, and he made a point of going there at lunchtime.

The day at the Center ran according to its usual rhythm, though with a certain anxiousness in light of the approaching date for the "silent majority's" coup.

Lídice, as always, brought rolls of fabric to paint banners, posters, paints, paste, twine and other materials for propaganda. As always, she'd look over to the door to the offices. Her quick glances gave rise to different interpretations. Did she fear or desire meeting David, from whom she had separated some months before?

Surprise. At the exact moment she was looking, David, dragging his leg, opened the door to leave.

It was a strange encounter. Passing by one another, they stopped and drew close until they were face to face eyeing one another in silence. It was most unusual behavior—neither even said hello. They didn't shake hands. But then spontaneously they reached out and held hands, right to left, left to right, and remained standing like that for a few moments without a word. In that instant they must have recalled the life they had shared in common. Then they let go their hands and Lídice walked away quickly.

Thinking the offices empty, Cremilde found her bent over the table, her head between her arms and sobbing.

"What's the matter, dear?"

Still crying, Lídice raised her head and looking at her responded, "You know, comrade, it was the right thing to do to separate. But it hurts a lot living without him."

Gabriel returned to the Center pleased, but when he walked into the Center some bad news awaited him.

Grandmother had gone there and spoken with David. Rita had disappeared from the house. This was already not the first time. She spent a night or two away, two or three days. But Grandmother learned that with other youngsters of the neighborhood, she got involved with little nighttime adventures making bonfires on the beaches and coming back home all dirty and disheveled. This time it had been eight days since she was gone, and she knew nothing of her.

"What?" Gabriel reacted. "It's been eight days and only now she tells me?"

What could he do? The next morning he had one meeting booked after another. But he ran to talk with Grandmother.

She received him right away with complaints. Rita was hanging around with bad company. She wasn't going to school. Now she only wanted to go out dressed in pants like a gang member with patches and rips going down to a handsome pair of white sports shoes. Grandmother had already spoken with a young girl living in the same street, a friend of Rita's in her little adventures. But the girl said she knew nothing, nor had any idea where to find her.

"I'll go talk with her," said Gabriel.

"She won't tell you anything. Those people are no good."

"Tell me where she lives."

"She's always running around the street with her friends." Telling him to come with her to the window, she pointed to a cluster of young people sitting on the ground some fifty meters away. "She's that one there with the yellow shirt."

Gabriel left and went over to the group, pointing to Rita's friend. "Come here."

The girl shrugged her shoulders and didn't move. But Gabriel persisted, so she got up and approached him.

He introduced himself as Rita's father and managed to convince her. The girl provided the address of one of Rita's friends, who maybe would know where she was.

Gabriel went to that street and house number immediately, to a building old and sad. At the entrance he smelled the odor of fish frying in rancid oil. Cartons and boxes were randomly stacked. Up three steps and he knocked on the door.

"Who's there?" someone asked from inside. It was the coarse voice of a woman.

"Is Janeto there?"

The response was slow in coming, with a long silence. Again came the woman's voice, gruff and aggressive. "What do you want with him?"

"I'm a friend. I just need a minute."

"What do you want with him?" the woman repeated.

Another silence followed. Finally the lock turned, and an angry, shocked face appeared in the crack of a half-open doorway.

"What do you want with him?" she said once again.

"Take it easy, I've come for a good reason," Gabriel tried to reassure her.

The woman hesitated, then called out, "Janeto!"

The boy came, his hair ruffled, a charming adolescent face with a tired aspect, his silky beard in need of a shave, his eyes with a strange brilliant gloss. He stood still, waiting for the visitor to explain himself.

The woman retreated a short distance to observe.

"I'm Rita's father, and I'd like to talk with you."

"I'll be right back," the boy said, pushing the woman aside and disappearing into the interior of the house. The woman closed the door, and Gabriel heard the voices of an argument. Her voice was raised, as she spoke rapidly and nervously. The boy's voice was lower and calmer.

After a while, the door opened again.

"Watch what you're getting yourself into!" the mother yelled from inside, more nervous than scolding.

The boy joined Gabriel outside. Gabriel explained why he had come. That he was Rita's father, and it had been several days since she had disappeared from her house. He had looked everywhere, knocked on many doors, and no one knew anything. Finally someone had mentioned him, saying he was her daughter's friend. Maybe he knew something.

The boy shook his head, visibly considering what response to give. "Bottom line, what do you want?"

"Just to find out how she is, that's all."

The boy thought a few more moments. "Come with me," he said decisively.

And with that he stepped out to the street. He brought Gabriel to the flea market and walked around talking with this one and that one. "I don't know anything yet, but I can find out. She's got to be in the Algarve. Go have lunch and we'll meet here at two, okay?"

They separated, but the boy came back. "Do you have a car?" he asked.

"I'll get one," Gabriel answered, not knowing how he'd find it.

He told Marco what was happening and that he wanted to look for his daughter. That he needed a car.

"No," said Marco. It was impossible to loan out for two days the car he got around in. And he almost reprimanded him.

"How can you, in this situation, a few days out from the coup, abandon what you have to do? Can't you wait until the 28th?"

It was just for that afternoon, Gabriel said with determination. He'd be back the next morning.

"We're in a critical moment. Even with all our forces, we're still very few. If anything should happen to you, you do know what that would mean, don't you?"

"Maybe I shouldn't do it," Gabriel responded. For the Party he had always been capable of giving his life. But he was also capable of giving it for the future of his daughter. He couldn't abandon her in this hour of danger. He wouldn't desert her. He had to find her.

Marco did not loan the car he drove. He had already said all he had to say about that. But he mentioned another comrade, telephoned him to come urgently to the Center and asked him to loan Gabriel his car. With no questions asked, and without knowing what it was for, he loaned it. "Now watch out you don't crash it."

Unaware of what a dramatic hour Gabriel was passing through, and joking around as he always did, the owner of the car commented further, "My concern is not for you. It's for the car!

"If you die, okay, you're dead and that's that. But my car, if I'm left without it, how am I going to live my life?"

And as though fearing that what he had just said would be taken in the wrong spirit, he slapped Gabriel on the shoulder and added, "Don't worry. Have a good trip, comrade."

Chapter *13*

At the agreed time, Janeto was there waiting. Already behind the steering wheel, Gabriel suggested, "Let's stop by your house to let your mother know."

"Not necessary," Janeto mumbled.

"But let's just stop for a second and we'll get on our way. By car we'll be there in a jiff."

"Not necessary," Janeto repeated. "She's used to it."

They got to the Algarve in late afternoon and aimed for a little fishing village. Janeto had him stop near the beach, told him to wait and disappeared down a back street.

Janeto took his time. In his rush to know something of Rita, Gabriel began to get anxious and irritated.

In the end, he barely knew Janeto. He recalled his mother's nervousness, the way she warned, "Watch what you're getting yourself into!" and above all those strange eyes of his as if coated with varnish...drugs, obviously.

An idea occurred to him. He felt a little ashamed of himself for it, but it kept popping into his mind, all the more stubbornly the longer Janeto was away. What if the boy had taken advantage of a ride to the Algarve and not to find Rita?

The image kept coming back to him of those shining eyes of a druggie. On the other hand, Janeto seemed to be diligent and sincere. Gabriel wound up feeling his doubts recede and his confidence winning.

It was good that he had come to that conclusion. Janeto returned. "I figured out where she is. Let's go!"

They found her on the main street of a nearby city, selling handicrafts spread out on the ground. Rita was painting a small stone. Sitting next to her, a young man with a bored, indifferent expression was petting a dog.

"Danilo," Janeto said in a tone that sounded more like an order, "take Rita's father to the tent. I want him to see her there."

And with that, he took his leave and disappeared without coming back.

Rita barely greeted her father. She seemed annoyed and said nothing when she heard Janeto's order. They picked up the handicrafts and started walking. Danilo continued to pet the dog.

When they got to the tent, on a depressing, empty lot, Gabriel kissed his daughter and said he had come to find her.

"I'm staying!" she replied, angry and confrontational. Maybe she was unhappy with herself.

Squatting by her side, Danilo petted the dog with a mechanical gesture, uncommunicatively. He appeared indifferent to what was taking place. A few meters away a boy with a blue band tied around his head stood observing the scene with an innocent, indecipherable smile.

"My daughter—" Gabriel pressed.

Three times Rita gave the same response. "I'm staying! I already told you I'm staying."

As the twilight advanced, a thin drizzle, light and silent, began to fall. As night came on, the lot became more deserted, and the isolation of those three young people even sadder.

Gabriel did not take his eyes off Rita's face—fine, beautiful, childlike, and yet firmly fixed in bitter determination.

He approached closer to his daughter, gave her a kiss and straightened himself up. Then he gave her some money, which she took.

Danilo went on petting the dog, the other boy standing stock still. Gabriel bent over again to kiss his daughter.

"Let us know how you are, okay?" And he said goodbye, his chest crushed by anguish and distress.

Maybe he himself did not appreciate that the depth of despair over the fate and future of those we love is the exact measure of the love we have for them.

"Let us hear from you," he said again.

"Okay," Rita whispered, now in a low, calm, even friendly voice.

From a few steps away, in such pain and possessed by infinite sadness, Gabriel looked at the group he was leaving. The three youngsters there had no clue of the typhoon of feelings practically strangling him with stinging wretchedness.

He was already standing by the car when the boy with the blue headband came alive and burst over to him, placed himself before him, and revealed the restless child he truly was. "Take me to Lisbon," he all but implored.

The request hurt Gabriel even more by contrast with Rita staying there, lost in a wilderness, in the falling mist in the dark of night alongside a boy who seemed oblivious to everything around him.

"Do you really want to come?"

The boy nodded yes, and without any further question opened the car door and slid into the back seat.

Gabriel glanced back once more. Next to the tent, insignificant, abandoned in that deserted place, Danilo never stopped petting the dog and Rita maintained her same expression. He couldn't tell if she raised her gaze to meet his.

Once in the car, before putting it in gear, Gabriel turned to look at the boy. He had curled up in the back, his head between his arms. Maybe he was already asleep.

The car started off and within a few minutes, having traversed the rough byways through the countryside, entered onto the main highway.

Night fell, and the car swerved around the mountainous curves—curve after curve after curve without end. Gabriel drove as if on automatic. The obstinate image he had before his eyes, agonizing and exact, was that of the insignificant tent on a vacant lot, the twilight, the soft rain, Rita crouching and unmovable, and Danilo petting the dog. Now they were all surely in darkness, in the void, as though abandoned to the world.

The car conquered one curve after another zigzagging through the sierra, occasionally scraping the curb, other times weaving into the other lane. Gabriel performed his corrections smoothly and naturally, with a squeal of the tires that he paid no attention to.

With the sierra in the rearview mirror, now on the descent, the serpentine road started evening out until suddenly they were traveling straight lines across the Alentejo plain.

Exhausted, Gabriel pulled the car over to the side of the road to rest for a few minutes. Turning around expecting to see the boy asleep, he found him awake, leaning on the front seat, right next to him, almost touching the back of his neck. In the shadow he imagined that delicate, childlike face below the blue band around his head.

"Did you sleep?" he asked. "Do you actually want to go back home? I'll take you there," said Gabriel, eager to do for the boy what he had not been able to do for his daughter.

The boy signaled yes with his head and remained quiet.

Along the course of an endless straight road, all of a sudden appeared the bright shine of headlights from a long caravan of cars. These headlights were strange not only for their quantity but for the way they were deployed on the road. They traveled closer and closer together and passed by in a noisy hurricane of motors and metal. It was a column of armored cars and Jeeps.

"What nastiness are they up to?" Gabriel murmured.

In the deep darkness of the plain that enveloped the highway, he envisioned the revolution that was overtaking towns and villages, the workers who had started occupying and cultivating fallow lands, and he wondered too about the sabotage and violent offensive by the landowners.

The boy seemingly took no notice of the scene. "Did you see them?" Gabriel asked.

He didn't answer the question. What he did say, slowly and calmly was, however, an opening to converse. "I'm José."

He was no longer the unknown boy with the blue band around his forehead and scalp. He was the friend who invited another to know him, and who offered his friendship and confidence.

"I'll take you home," Gabriel repeated. "Where do you live?"

Now the boy responded quickly. "In Lumiar."

Then, as though he had said all he needed to say, he released his hold on the front seat and curled up again in the back to sleep. The trip continued monotonously, as before.

Confirming Gabriel's train of thought, a reddish glow appeared in the distance, softening the darkness. Far off at first, it took on greater dimension as the car proceeded along his endless straight course. He knew that in Alentejo, Joaquina's homeland, as her brother had also reported, the latifundists had set fire to forests and even to their crops. This was certainly one more instance of it.

They came into Lisbon, still night. The streets had an unusual animation about them. Groups of people, some of them with banners, were rushing to get where they were going.

Gabriel stopped the car at the Campo Grande. The boy was still sleeping.

"José!"

The boy sat up, shuddering with the early morning cool, and wiped his eyes and face.

"Where do you want me to leave you? What street?"

Met by silence, he repeated his questions. Another pause followed.

"I'm not going!" the youth finally said in a quiet but desperate voice, just as Rita had spoken when she said, "I'm staying!"

"You had said—"

"I'm not going!" he repeated. And saying nothing more, he opened the back door, got out and disappeared into the gardens of Campo Grande.

Gabriel remained parked there, as if waiting for José to come back, but he didn't. It was already dawning, and he placed the car in gear and headed for the Party Center.

The Center was full of comrades who had spent the night there, some seated on the Center's few chairs around the tables, others standing, others still sleeping, sitting or huddled on the floor.

"Where's Marco?" he asked.

"He spent the night with us. He's in his office."

Gabriel went in to see him. The expression on Gabriel's face looked so sorrowful that Marco didn't even ask.

"You spent the whole night driving—must have been more than seven hundred kilometers. Go rest a little."

"This is no time for sleeping, Marco. Staying up nights is what you do, it's what David does, it's what Matilde does, it's what thousands of comrades are doing these days. So I'm here to do my work."

"All right then, have a seat. There's good news for everyone. The bus drivers and truck drivers have declared a strike."

"That's significant, but we might have hoped for more from the labor movement," Gabriel observed, forcing himself to pay attention, but sensing the irresistible droop of his eyelids.

"The ones I mentioned," Marco went on, "are the ones that have declared a strike for the 27th and 28th. But many others have condemned the threatening announcement to march on Lisbon."

Those who had declared their opposition were the telecommunications union, the chemical workers, the merchant marine. Even the professional soccer players union got on board—so people wouldn't take up the provocative public offer of free rides to Lisbon to anyone who wanted to attend a soccer match that a club from the North was holding in Lisbon that same day, the 28th.

"That's important," Gabriel commented, without any follow-up to the conversation. Both of them remained silent for another minute.

"There's something else I want to discuss with you. David's not here and I want to hear your opinion. I already heard Matilde's."

Returning from a function in the city where she was the speaker, Matilde was editing a manifesto aimed at the population of the parish. She was going to make a mimeograph stencil, print it out and distribute it personally to the people of the old quarter.

Gabriel tried to listen so he could give the opinion being asked of him. But for any person, nature is stronger than what they themselves judge it to be. His eyelids were falling heavily. He opened his eyes again, listened some more as Marco's voice became ever more faint, and suddenly he saw himself on a vast plain stretching out to a far horizon. And on the ground there were some unfamiliar fruits he was trying to pick up—"

"Gabriel, excuse me, but if I didn't grab you, you would have fallen out of your chair," Marco said, as he straightened him up.

"Excuse *me*, Marco. This is the second time it's happened as I was talking with someone. I suddenly fall asleep."

"Don't think you're the only one, Gabriel." The same thing had occurred with him. Just a few days before, he was in his office working, and a comrade was all talk, talk, talk, and suddenly, just as it happened with Gabriel, he saw himself together with a bunch of friends—who weren't there, of course—and he even remembered some of the words they were saying in his dream.

"Yeah, so it goes. But it was so brief that the comrade kept talking without realizing that anything had happened. Well, at least I think so."

"Wait a minute, I'll be right back," said Gabriel. He stood up and left.

In the washroom he grabbed a towel, placed it under the faucet until it was soaked, and when he returned to the office he wrapped it around his head. He cut an odd figure. Marco, who was always so serious, couldn't help laughing. "It suits you well," he joked ironically.

"I'm ready, you can go on," Gabriel said.

"A good prescription," Marco said, staring at his friend Gabriel with a wet towel tied to his skull.

Marco went back a little in what he had said, because Gabriel had not heard everything.

When Joaquina arrived, they had a couple of coffees. And the day proceeded like the ones before.

Chapter 14

When Zé Manuel was walking to the Center, some hundred meters away he noticed two men wearing dark sunglasses observing the street from the entranceway to a building. When they saw him, they retreated inside. Zé Manuel cut through an alley and took a stroll through the neighborhood for a good hour before returning to the Center along the same street.

The two men were still there, but now on the sidewalk as if having a conversation, yet not walking anywhere.

I have to find out if this is about us, he thought.

And to kill some more time, he set out on a long hike through the city. The agitation in the streets had grown more fervid than in the previous days.

On one empty street a group was painting an enormous panel on a white wall, in beautiful full color, of workers with red flags in a mass demonstration.

Cars with right-wing banners circulated through the streets. You could see a certain nervousness in the way people walked, with quick steps indicating awareness that a great threat was closing in.

On the way to the Center, on the sloping street that led to the old quarter, a car passed him down the incline inexplicably slowly, the occupants watching the street from side to side. What were they looking for in this neighborhood where they were strangers?

On the little side street that led directly to the Center, again he saw the men with the dark glasses, now with a woman with whom they seemed to be conversing.

The time before, they hadn't fixed their eyes directly on him. Now he saw them clearly turning their heads in his direction.

When he got to the Center, he found Luís. "They're surveilling the Center. They're getting ready for something." They went to get some coffee.

Zé Manuel left the Center, and Luís joined his security team who were waiting for him in their usual corner of the reception hall.

Many comrades practically lived at the Center, accommodating themselves as they might.

Corporal Santos, always seen with his military shirt, used the lull to continue telling his story. He had already explained why he had rebelled against the colonial war. He reminded his listeners about the massacre of the population of a village—men, women and children— the way they set fire to the humble huts they lived in, and then the Portuguese soldiers laughing with the Black heads spiked on bayonets. It was then that he decided to desert, and he did. He retreated into the bush, always afraid of wild animals and snakes. He walked west to reach the ocean, and that's how he reached the port of Benguela.

"Sounds like a tall story," Rudolfo interrupted. "How did you cross Angola without eating, without water, and unable to protect yourself from the sun?"

He ate dried fruits, drank water wherever he found it, and took refuge from the sun under trees along the way.

"You're lying," Rudolfo insisted.

"You don't ever want to go through what I went through," said Corporal Santos.

"I believe you," Luís declared. He was also in the war and had seen even more horrible and shocking things.

At the port of Benguela, Corporal Santos continued, he was able to get a Norwegian boat to take him aboard on the voyage to France. There he worked very hard, in the worst-paid jobs that the French refused to do—garbage removal, public works, sewer cleaning. He'd lived under bridges or in slums with tin shacks, because they have those in France too—"

Here Rudolfo broke in as he had the other times. "More lies!" He rose and took himself over to the bar to have a beer.

"It's a shame," the narrator said. "He left not hearing the best and the worst of these stories about our lives as soldiers."

Apart from the many comrades who spent the night at the Center, there were only Rudolfo and Luís for security.

In the middle of the night, Luís was sitting at a table reading, and Rudolfo was drinking at the bar when they heard a strange noise coming from the offices inside. They went to the door that opened onto the corridor and listened carefully. The sound was coming not from the offices, but from the door at the end of the corridor that opened to the street. Someone was obviously trying to break in.

"Let's make some noise," Luís proposed. "Let's both shout, and whoever it is will certainly run away."

"No," Rudolfo said, remembering Zé Manuel's warning. "If they want to break in by force, we need to give them a lesson."

Step by careful step they tiptoed down the corridor, stood by the offices and waited. By the sounds coming from the door, it was clearly not anyone from the Center. They tried in vain to open the lock. It seemed they also tried to insert a crowbar under the door. The operation took longer than they probably expected.

"They aren't thieves," Luís whispered. "They've got to be provocateurs."

Having seen the two guards enter the corridor and take their time coming back, one of the comrades overnighting in the reception also went to see if they might need something. He opened the door to the corridor and light from the reception hall came in. In the shadows he saw Luís and Rudolfo and heard the sound coming from the entry door.

"Shhhh," said Luís in a barely audible voice, and without a word he gestured the comrade to go back to reception and close the door.

Finally the outside door gave in. Three men, one with a flashlight in hand, started walking down the corridor.

They didn't get farther than a few steps. Suddenly Rudolfo threw the lights on and fell on top of them, while Luís, in a split second, almost as if he were flying, jumped on the one holding a pistol, wresting it out of his hands before he had time to shoot. They beat the intruders so badly that when they threw them out to the street, not one of them was left standing. Only with difficulty did they manage to get up and stumble off into the dark.

The two comrades reinstalled the broken door the best they could, returned to reception, and went back to where they had been before—Rudolfo at the counter drinking beer (how many, no one knows), and Luís seated at a table reading.

The comrade who had gone to the corridor to check on them approached Luís. "Anything happen?"

"No, comrade. Everything's okay," and Luís went on reading.

As she always did, Joaquina arrived in the early morning. They told her what had happened.

"Bravo, boys," she smiled. "Luís, have another coffee on me. And you, Rudolfo, congratulations for what you did. But today you're not drinking here any more, 'cause you look pretty soaked already. Why don't you go out if you want?"

That's how the day began at the Party Center of Santa Efigénia. When Marco came, they told him what had occurred. Luís handed over the pistol he had seized.

The incident was reported to the Regional Committee. That same night similar events had taken place at other Party Centers. At one, before the intruders were chased off, they had succeeded in gaining access to an office, where they searched drawers and cabinets. Trying to find compromising documents? Looking for weapons?

Demonstrably, this was not the work of thieves, but a concerted counter-revolutionary operation on the eve of a coup by the "silent majority."

When he found out about the event, one older comrade at the Center commented, "Rudolfo's our real hero. I don't even get why we have a little spring chicken like Luís on security."

Another comrade, rather more prudently, tried to explain. "I think in his spare time he learned martial arts." More daringly, the first chance he got, he posed the question directly: "Come on, Luís, tell us. Do you practice karate?"

Luís chuckled, but didn't say anything.

Meanwhile, in contrast with these disturbing developments, there also came news of meetings and demonstrations in many cities and towns throughout the country.

Berta was even given the task of taking notes on all this news and preparing a report as soon as possible to evaluate the degree of popular mobilization.

"Hey, Berta, how's your research going?" Nelo asked her.

"You want to know more than you should, my dear. When I've finished my work I'll hand it to our leadership."

All day long, work proceeded vigorously at the Santa Efigénia Center. The comrades reached out in a variety of ways to the people of the parish.

The 28th was rapidly approaching now. Neither the government, nor COPCON, nor the president of the Republic were taking measures to impede the coup in progress.

A meeting of huge proportions took place in Lisbon. Marco, Gabriel, David, Matilde and the Party members in the parish worked tirelessly. During those days they slept little if they slept at all.

Day by day there were signs of a very broad willingness to help stop the entry into Lisbon of the gigantic "silent majority" demonstration. Reactionary elements announced plans to give full executive power to the president, declare the PCP illegal, and send leaders of the Party and the leftist military to prison.

Counter-revolutionary activity turned aggressive at every turn: insults, threats, assaults, attacks, violent opposition to actions on behalf of the Party, the unions, the youth, and broad democratic sectors, all acts that showed the reactionaries' confidence in winning. And now a new demonstration of their tactics, the planned simultaneous attacks on the Party Centers such as in Santa Efigénia Parish.

At the same time, the Party and youth groups were conducting daily work all over the city, distributing manifestos in the streets and at the front entrances to factories, going door to door talking with the population and driving around in a few cars equipped with loud-speakers. Without rest, Matilde organized meetings with the young people at her school and with the residents of her neighborhood, explaining the current highly dangerous situation.

All this mobilization constituted a prod to resist and fight. The activists inevitably encountered fear and anxiety. But in general they believed it was going to be possible to halt the march on Lisbon and cut off entrances to the city.

"We'll be there!" said the workers at the doors to their workplaces.

Chapter 15

Not far from the Party Center the narrow street ran down an incline from the old city. Mornings, an ants nest of people walked from the heights of the neighborhood down to their jobs. And at night, after the residents retuned home, it was silent and deserted.

The young comrades went along the street pasting posters on the building walls, serious and pleased, accomplishing their mission.

Out of the blue, the violent roar of a car rocketing up the street rumbled through the air. They barely had time to look around to see what it was, when the noise came nearer and nearer, louder and louder. The car sped past them like a tornado and disappeared from sight at the top of the hill.

"Did you see that?" Nelo shouted. "It's a Jaguar!"

How strange to see a car like that in the neighborhood, and at such a ferocious speed. Where could it be going? The road gave out up ahead in a community of old houses.

"This has to do with us. The guys will be here soon," said Zé Manuel.

"Let's not do anything rash," Berta yelled. "Let's finish up—there's just a few posters left."

They hurried to complete their work. When they thought they'd imagined hearing a false alarm, the Jaguar reappeared, now descending the street slowly and silently.

As it came close, it speeded up, revving its engine, and in a sharp squeal of rubber in a sudden brake, it stopped suddenly right in front of the young activists.

At that moment, Zé Manuel didn't ask anything of anyone, but took off fast and disappeared through a by-street.

"Hey, he's escaping," one of the youth protested.

"Zé Manuel is not escaping," Nelo corrected him.

The truth of Zé Manuel's "escape" would be revealed shortly. He had anticipated an imminent attack and run to seek reinforcement. It was a correct decision, in the right place at the right time.

In an instant, obviously commanded by a strong guy in a garishly colored shirt, three more men got out of the Jaguar and started attacking with clubs, kicking over the cans of paint and paste, hitting the youth with uncontrolled fury. They shoved, punched and beat, all the time screaming insults. "Out of here, you bastards! Go back to your mommies!" the one in the garish shirt yelled.

The youth fought back courageously and no one tried to flee. They would have been massacred when the skirmish had just begun, if reinforcements from the Party Center, led by Zé Manuel, hadn't come to the scene via that by-street. A large number had arrived and encircled the provocateurs, not allowing them any room to move.

The one in the colored shirt and one other hefty, powerful guy tried to break through the circle. They knocked a few comrades down, but ended up immobilized like wounded bulls in the ring.

One of them pulled out a pistol, but before he could fire it, he too was surrounded and squeezed in by a human ring that immobilized and disarmed him.

The skirmish ended and the comrades now demanded that the aggressors identify themselves. Refusing to do so, and gesticulating wildly, spewing curses, they struggled in vain to break through the human ring that had captured them.

The argument proceeded with both sides shouting. "We're not letting you go. You're arrested!" one comrade yelled.

Another declared, "You have no excuse for being here, so come with us to the police station."

"Who are you to take us prisoner?" the man in the colored shirt bellowed. And in their rage they still tried to force their way out.

Finally, they had no choice but to give in.

"And the car? We can't leave it here."

"It'll be fine," Berta said. "Someone will take care of it," she added, laughing.

So they were marched several streets away to the nearest police station, in the midst of a throng of neighbors who had joined the parade.

A substantial crowd surrounded the front door of the police station.

As soon as they entered, things started to go badly for the five comrades—only five that the police allowed to accompany the prisoners.

"You say you arrested them," the station chief mocked the young comrades. "What authority do you have to arrest anyone?"

Because the attackers were fascists. They'd come in a group. They'd started the assault, and had threatened with firearms.

"But are you the police, or what?" the chief interrupted with irritation. And he repeated: "You can't just arrest anyone. If you do, it's you who are infringing on the law. And besides, it was you who were violating the law by gluing posters on buildings."

"But they're fascists!" one of the five yelled. "It's your obligation to identify them."

"Fascists? Repeat that to me, you commie!" the man in the colored shirt yelled back, and he gave the youth a violent shove.

"Stop that," was all the police chief commented with an unconcerned air.

One of the detained, a man sporting a thick chamois leather jacket, pulled the chief over to a corner with unexpected familiarity and showed him a card. The chief looked at the card and handed it back without a word, and the two returned to join the others.

The arrested provocateurs and the five comrades who had come into the station with them were all under watch by three silent guards.

Out on the street hundreds of people coming down from the old city and others who had joined up with them were protesting.

The station chief disappeared into an inner office, staying so long it seemed he would not return. But he did, with a nonchalant attitude as though nothing had happened.

"All right, you can go," he said to the five comrades.

"And them?"

"They're staying here."

If they were actually to be taken prisoner that would be satisfactory, but that was highly doubtful.

"So we leave, and then the guy tells them to leave too, and we don't ever find out who they are."

"You can go," the chief said again.

Out on the street, the large mass of demonstrators, seeing the comrades come out, believed the others remained under arrest. There were applause, words of congratulations and shouts of joy. Under the circumstances, nothing more could be done.

"Fascists! Fascists!" they shouted.

Meanwhile, a Military Police jeep had parked outside. They were told what the demonstration was all about and the soldiers kept the peace as events unfolded, conversing with the people.

"After all, the bad guys have been arrested," someone said.

One of the soldiers replied, "You handed the bad guys over to the police. But it won't be long before they're let go."

"You can be sure of it," another soldier added. "Those guys in the police station are all involved in the coup."

"There's nothing else for us to do here," someone else said.

The demonstrators stayed on the street for another good hour, but then started dispersing. Only a few curious ones remained silently in front of the police station.

Over the next few days, the provocations, attacks and acts of violence increased. The reactionaries acted without restraint—not from the police, nor the National Guard, nor any soldiers from COPCON. It became impossible to move around by night.

In the early morning a piece of sad news came to the Center. The information was vague, but Zé Manuel had been taken to the hospital.

Only hours later did the reason become known. In the lower area of the parish the fascists had mounted an ambush for a well-known intellectual. And it was he who ultimately related what happened. A bunch of these fascists surrounded him and started hurling insults at him and pushing him around. "Commie son of a bitch. If you're so brave, show us now."

A very young fellow was coming from the other direction and was going to pass by them. But what could he do? Even eye witnesses during those days couldn't do much of anything.

The argument heated up, the insults grew more violent in tone, and the victim of the attack tried to react. One of the assailants pulled out a pistol, certainly to kill him.

At that point Zé Manuel, who was now quite near the group, jumped in one leap on the guy holding the pistol. Some shots were fired. Zé Manuel fell to the ground, and the victim of the assault, taking advantage of the attackers' surprise, ran off in the dark of night. And with that unforeseen outcome, the provocateurs vanished too.

Zé Manuel lay on the ground unconscious. Only in the morning did they find him. Someone brought him to the hospital. But they couldn't do anything for him there. He was dead.

Chapter *16*

Leaders of the Party Center met to evaluate the situation and the measures to be taken.

Gabriel was in a good mood and worry-free. Grandmother had just telephoned to say that Rita had returned home. Marco showed signs of extreme fatigue but maintained his capacity for analyzing problems. David exhibited his usual energy, as though he hadn't done anything special the day before. Matilde was the eternal optimist.

The evening before, Marco had been summoned to a meeting which, he told his comrades, was called to consider the concrete possibilities and means of cutting off the march on Lisbon. "It was a very useful meeting," he stated.

Present at that meeting were comrades from all the Party Centers in Lisbon, union leaders, Party leaders from all the regional committees around the capital—Vila Franca, Loures, Oeiras—and also delegates from the regional organization in Setúbal.

The picture was truly grave. Contradictory news reports from uncertain sources were coming in to Lisbon from all over the country.

"As far as that's concerned, it would be good if you could sharpen our communications," David suggested.

"Naturally. I will," Marco answered.

The decisive battle, in most people's expectations, would occur at the gates of Lisbon.

At the meeting, one comrade in the leadership, a new member with a quiet voice, started saying there was extremely troubling news, as well as other more encouraging news.

"It would help us if you could give a more precise idea of both one and the other," said David.

"I can do that," Marco responded. About the troubling news, it was hard to believe what was in fact already known. The means of transportation that had been chartered to bring demonstrators for free had mounted to inconceivable numbers. From Porto, they were talking about five hundred buses. Three hundred from Braga, two hundred from Aveiro, three hundred from Viseu and so on from north to south. Add them up and buses alone with free transportation would bring more than a hundred thousand demonstrators to Lisbon supporting the coup. On top of that, special free chartered trains, tens of thousands of cars and even special flights on TAP, the national airline.

The government was paralyzed and not taking action. COPCON seemed indifferent: Responding to a Party initiative, one official said, "It's a dispute among civilians, and the civilians will have to resolve it."

The Party needed a correct assessment of the situation in order to prepare its response. It direly needed to prevent the planned march on Lisbon and the demonstration supporting the president's appeal to assume power and "save the country" from communism. The comrades believed that for the coup not to advance, they couldn't count on the government, nor on COPCON, and not even on the military of the MFA. They had concluded that only one solution existed: The people, even if unarmed, had to impede the entry into Lisbon on the one hand, and on the other, prevent or discourage buses and other means of transportation from leaving.

As to that, inspiring news was coming in—the rising consciousness of workers and the people overall about the dangers of a coup, and the determination to do everything possible to stop the buses from departing and to cut off the access roads into Lisbon.

Interrupting his report, Marco observed that "It all depends on us. Politically, we were never so alone. And never before has our Party had such broad approval and support from the masses in such a decisive battle."

He continued his analysis. The delegate from the Setúbal district had guaranteed that they would not allow the ferryboats to depart from Cacilhas or Seixal, and they would cut off the bridge traffic over the Tagus and the access to the Vila Franca bridge at both Alcochete and Porto Alto.

One thing looked certain to everyone. "Either we, with the masses, cut off their passage," Marco stated, "or the counter-revolutionary coup will go on to success."

A proposal came to the floor. Little time remained.

"Just two days," Gabriel said.

"So it's been decided: to make a survey of all the entrances to Lisbon—the main ones and the alternative ones as well," Marco continued.

At each point they would examine the strategic places where to set up roadblocks and not allow any transportation into the city. They would also expand this study to the Party committees in Sintra and

Cascais, for roadblocks there, even far away from the gates of Lisbon, could contain the counter-revolutionary demonstrators.

To coordinate this work and ensure the execution of the plan on the 27th, with the inevitable need for last-minute corrections, a small committee of comrades who knew the region well was chosen, Marco himself among them. Each one would have a car at his disposal.

They considered it critical to establish an immediate linkup with the railroad workers at the Entroncamento rail node north of Lisbon.

Now, informed about what had been decided, they analyzed the situation. "This meeting," David observed, "confirmed what we have been thinking for a long time."

There wasn't much time to spare before the date of the march on Lisbon.

"There's just one thing to do," David went on, "here in the parish as in the whole capital and the whole country: Mobilize the masses."

Marco concurred. "It's absolutely necessary to mobilize the general population. And for that it's our Party and only our Party, with the unions, that is in a position to attempt this mobilization and defeat the coup."

"If our Party fails—" Gabriel began.

"It will not fail!" David interrupted him.

The way things stood, either they succeeded to stop the demonstration or a new dictatorship and the violent repression of the Party and the left military would follow.

"In Santa Efigénia Parish," Matilde said with conviction, "the people are ready to intervene and get mobilized."

They felt certain that the same was also true in the rest of the city. Lisbon was committed to not allowing the "silent majority" to enter. They would do what they needed to deploy the popular forces and effectively cut off the roads leading into the city.

They divided up the assignments. Marco, according to the resolution from the previous night, would participate in managing the mounting of roadblocks.

"As far as the old quarter goes, leave that to me," Matilde offered.

David would take charge of the Center and everything taking place there, and of the preparation for setting out to the roadblocks. Gabriel took over the task of leading people from the parish to the places they were assigned.

Chapter *17*

The morning of the 27th dawned with the Party Center full of comrades who had spent the night there, seated on the couple of dozen chairs, standing, or even stretched out on the floor. They felt ready for action, ready with the power of an unarmed people to stop the dangerous coup at the highest ranks of the State.

Meanwhile, baseless rumors confused a lot of people. One that ran through the city had it that the president had called for a provocative massing of people against the prime minister in the bull ring.

One rightist in Santa Efigénia kept defending the coup. He repeated the reactionary argument that it was a legal initiative legitimated by two democratic parties. And that one couldn't prevent a demonstration whose legitimacy had been established by the 25th of April.

Against the stream of the general attitude of combativeness, here and there some other voices could be heard.

"The government is just waiting for the right time to intervene," some said.

"The head of COPCON will step in when it's appropriate," said others.

Pure illusions. The civil and military authorities, the government and COPCON, seemed to have disappeared—or were in connivance.

In the last few days the president revealed his arrogance by announcing in advance what he considered a sure victory.

One attempt at a palace coup by his people had already failed in the first provisional government. Now he was convinced that this elegantly elaborated operation that he himself had shaped, supposedly without his fingerprints, would not fail. He thought of himself, after all, as a genius of a commander and a skilled politician.

Despite the anxiousness and uncertainty, a general feeling of confidence prevailed. For the promoters of the coup as much as for those who fought against it, the opinion was shared that the march on Lisbon, if victorious, would completely change the existing situation.

The operation suffered an important setback just days beforehand: The declaration of the demonstration's illegality and the seizure of some of the leaders of the march on Lisbon from the two fascist parties of ex-PIDE members and ex-legionnaires, which had been the official sponsors, as straw men. Those arrests, almost at the last minute, deprived the coup of some of its most active captains of the "silent majority" mobilization and of all the contrived provocations and acts of violence and terrorism.

"Finally it looks like the government is banning the demonstration," some optimists said as an echo to these developments.

There was indeed a declaration by the government. But it was so unauthorized and uncredited that the declaration had so little public resonance, was so weak and so late, that only days later did the newspapers get around to publishing it, and even then without giving it any importance.

Though the accepted view held that it was up to the unarmed population to stop the entry into Lisbon, many still had doubts and questions that were gradually being surmounted.

Two workers were talking:

"You can count on me. I'll be going to the blockades. But if they send thousands of buses full of people, will we—unarmed—will we have the power to stop them from coming into Lisbon?"

"Look, my friend," the other explained, "if you don't let the first one get through and more than a thousand come after, they'll be backed up for at least fifty kilometers, all stopped without being able to go forward or go back to try another way in."

In those days, as in the days preceding, the people's opposition found its impressive voice in the gatherings, meetings and demonstrations from north to south, showing their determination to fight.

"Demonstrations are just demonstrations," one comrade observed. "The consciousness and determination of the people all over the country is something different from cutting the march on Lisbon off at the pass with your bare hands."

"It's different, that's true," another comrade disagreed, "but those huge demonstrations show the preparedness to intervene, to mount roadblocks and stop the counter-revolutionaries' passage—and even better to prevent those hundreds of buses the coup chartered from departing."

News of those demonstrations had been encouraging. They had heard of more than a hundred thousand participants in Setúbal, Coimbra, and Porto—and uniquely in that city with the participation of the Socialist leaders.

From five to ten thousand turned out in Póvoa de Varzim, Aljustrel, Guimarães, Évora, Portimão and Pias. A thousand to five thousand came out in Famalicão, Moura, Aldeia Nova de São Bento, Lagoa, Ferreira do Alentejo, Silves, Tavira, and Alverca.

All this information, still imprecise coming from this and that place, but impressive overall, built confidence in the ability to stop the coup.

Charged with calculating the number of expected buses, Berta also came up with a corresponding number of demonstrators against the coup. She gathered all the news reports and ran to announce her first tally to David. "I've done the numbers, and you know what? From north to south more than four hundred thousand people demonstrated protesting the march on Lisbon."

"If your count is correct," David seemed pleased, "that shows our great capacity for mobilization."

"We have to act, and now!" Marco stressed to the committee assigned to organizing the blockades around Lisbon.

Rightwing demonstrators might start arriving. It was necessary to reinforce the vigilance at the principal access routes to the capital. With a significant concentration of people they would not allow passage to any suspect transportation.

At the end of the day of the 27th, some fresh and as yet unconfirmed but serious news arrived at the Party Center of Santa Efigénia Parish. The president had called a meeting of the Council of Ministers that evening.

"Certainly not to call off the demonstration and the coup," David calmly noted, and was right.

It later came to be learned that the president accused the government, under Communist influence, of opposing the announced national demonstration to support him. He threatened that "if the government does not take measures against the agitators who seek to impede the demonstration, I will take them myself." Thus he declared his intentions, for he well knew that the government would not accept his ultimatum, and he knew for certain the demonstration would take place.

The news spread like wildfire. The popular mobilization already in motion only stepped up its commitment.

It was nine o'clock that night. There was no time to lose.

At the jammed Party Center, everyone felt eager to proceed to their assigned posts.

Around nine-thirty, the instruction from the Central Committee came to the Center: Immediately launch the popular mobilization and mount the roadblocks at all the entrances, direct and indirect, to the city without delay. Don't wait another minute. The time has come.

The many comrades who for days had been ready to act left in groups for the access roads into the city. They set out without banners or signs. They didn't march in formation, but with a resolute, silent stride.

These were not demonstrations, but rather expeditions to meet a great battle. It must have been what everyone was thinking.

Along the way they encountered other groups walking in the same direction—like them, without signage and also silent.

And as they proceeded through the streets, the groups flowed together without any confusion as to the tasks given to each one.

And then, once all amassed, the groups separated out again. Some in the front headed for the Carriche Highway and nearby streets. Others struck out for the streets leading to Sacavém. And others went to the streets coming off the Pontinha.

Everyone was aware that if out across the country people had not cut off the "silent majority," it fell to them, the unarmed people, to stop them from entering Lisbon. And no one showed fear. There are situations in history where heroes tow the people behind them. Now the hero was the people themselves.

The group out of Santa Efigénia Parish integrated itself into the contingents sent to the Carriche Highway, where they would be given their assignments. Gabriel went with the group, also Nelo, Berta and Mila, Rudolfo and Corporal Santos. Inevitably, too, there was Isa ready to help with the hardest jobs.

Hiking toward the roadblocks, those with portable radios heard a succession of communiqués conveying joy and confidence. One union appealed ironically, though with clear directions, for people to come to a fair very early, at such-and-such an hour at a certain point on the outskirts of the city. Another union made a similar announcement for a fair somewhere else. The people with radios boasted about the novelty of their apparatus, and from them received even more of a prod to action.

Early in the morning they started hearing other communiqués. That an accord had been signed between the president, the government, the leftwing military and COPCON advising no opposition to the demonstration and all would remain as before. An accord between such forces was truly absurd when the battle was already engaged among them.

"Impossible! It's a provocation!" they shouted at the roadblocks. "Pay no attention! It's a provocation!"

Then came other communiqués no less strange, now from COPCON and its leader. That the situation was under control, that

COPCON had taken the necessary measures and therefore people should dismantle whatever blockades were still to be mounted. "Impossible!" people shouted to that too. "They haven't done anything up to now. And they're not going to do anything now either, right at the critical hour. Another provocation!"

"No one leave!" cried a voice from the middle of the crowd.

"No one leave!!" a multitude of voices picked up the slogan.

In one or two instances, soldiers appeared saying their orders were to lift the roadblocks, but they ended up working with the people putting them into place.

The directive went out to block off the streets. Never had such a vast popular mobilization been seen. The people *en masse* moved to cut off passage for the "silent majority." Gabriel and the others from Santa Efigénia Parish stood there at their positions.

Among the many young people participating Gabriel noticed one who was especially brazen. Skinny, moving fast, he placed himself on the front lines mounting the roadblocks. When the first cars appeared, side by side with other participants, he raised his arms and shouted, "Halt!"

And they all did. His companions made the drivers and the passengers park over to one side or remain in place subject to verification of documents and a search for weapons.

In all this coming and going a moment arrived when that young man came face to face with Gabriel. Small and very alert, he turned toward him with his eyes fixed on Gabriel. He had the delicate face of a child, a blue band wrapped tightly around his head.

"José!" It was the boy who a few weeks earlier had hitched a ride with him from the Algarve to Lisbon.

It was a brief instant, but without speaking, the boy expressed in that simple encounter with Gabriel all that he wanted to say. *See? I'm here!*

He took a few steps away, then stopped, turned about and said to Gabriel, "Rita and Janeto are here too somewhere!"

And then, in a rapid gesture indicating the crumbling, sandy ground, he took the stick he was carrying and quickly traced a long line in the sand. "They shall not pass here," he said with a seriousness contrasting with his almost childlike face.

Turning around, he disappeared swiftly into the avalanche of people who were preventing the "silent majority" from entering the capital. Far fewer buses showed up than expected. And all the roadblocks worked according to plan.

And over that line in the sand they did not pass.

Events like these go down in history like legends. But what is a legend if not a fantasy version of the truth?

At the hour when the reactionaries had announced that two hundred or three hundred thousand demonstrators should concentrate in front of the palace demanding that the president assume full powers, dismiss the government, dissolve the MFA and send the Communists packing, that whole vast space was completely empty.

Chapter 18

The people unarmed had just inflicted a mortal defeat to the conspiracies of the president and to a coup that would have been consummated in the palace square with an appeal from the country that he save it from Communism.

Lisbon had prepared itself to block the expected thousands of buses from getting through. But the victory was not only Lisbon's. From the news that came in, people all over the country had risen up against the danger. Stories had it that in many places the buses never even left. In other places they were held back by the blockades.

The railway workers at the Entroncamento made an important contribution, not permitting the special trains from the North to connect on to Lisbon. They searched every traveler, demanded to see identification, and confiscated weapons.

At one critical highway juncture in a town some fifty kilometers from Lisbon, people recalled the strong barriers they created with hundreds of participants. And all night long the locals ran back and forth bringing them bread, cheese, sausage, coffee and wine.

The coup was successfully defeated. Then a number of questions began to emerge.

Why was the president not immediately dismissed? Why did neither the government nor the armed forces appear to declare him fired? What was the meaning of the announcement that the president would make an address to the country, but only on the 30th? Why the delay of two days?—an inexplicable postponement.

Might someone suppose—as it later became known—that on the night of the 27th leading into the 28th, the president had summoned the head of the General Staff of the Armed Forces, the commander of COPCON and the Prime Minister to Belém and had kept them imprisoned there?

How could anyone believe the statement, which the people immediately rejected, with its incredible, impossible conclusion that the president, the government, the head of COPCON, and the Program Committee of the MFA all remained unchanged?

"Utter nonsense," people said at the blockades, hearing that morning on the radio the directives coming from Belém saying that as a result of this accord, there was no longer any reason for the roadblocks to exist.

Who could guess that, mortally defeated by the people, the president would try in those two days to mobilize loyal military units and impose by force the objectives he had failed to achieve with the "silent majority?" And that then he would annul the absurd compromise agreement he had announced and would launch, as revenge for the humiliating rout he had suffered, an offensive of pernicious violence against the PCP, the MFA and all those who had opposed him. His much vaunted strategic military genius had failed. His presumed political talent had also tanked.

Questions, doubts and distrust hung in the air. Despite the trouncing of the march in Lisbon, the blockades stayed up for those two days. What could the overpowered president say about it?

Only when it became clear that he did not have the support to claim victory through the armed forces loyal to him, only then, after his removal had been declared, did the roadblocks lift, although the people remained on guard.

No one individually could be cited as the victorious leader. The victory belonged to the people, to the masses.

During those days the Center was almost deserted. Everyone was still at the roadblocks. David stayed at the Center, radiant over the popular mobilization, the success of the strategy, and finally the victory. But his conclusions were more prudent.

"We won this battle, but the counter-revolution will be back. Let's celebrate this victory, but prepare for hard battles in the future."

The Party Center of Santa Efigénia Parish filled up again the next day, the people enjoying their happiness and renewed enthusiasm.

On the evening of the 30th they called an open plenary for the parish. Marco underscored the remarkable bravery of the victory they had achieved while, like David, warning of the real situation. "The counter-revolution will not retreat and will use whatever measures it can. We have to remain vigilant and continue the struggle."

David added, "With even more energy and more confidence."

The Party was now in a position to be the motor force behind the defense of the April Revolution. He went on to say that when it first distributed membership cards after the 25th of April, the Party had only four or five thousand members, and now had reached fifty thousand in the heat of battle. Every day new members were coming in and signing up.

The words were wise, and the warnings also wise without a doubt. But in those days the joy and ardor overcame any worries about the future.

During that short session the audience applauded a boy and girl who had just joined the Communist Youth.

But it was after the speeches that the happiness reached its height when a young musical group from the neighborhood introduced themselves. They came with their guitars and mandolins. They weren't from the Party but came to congratulate it and offer to play a little if the audience was interested.

The guitar music received a hearty hand. The vocalist sang a classic fado of love and sorrow.

One young comrade observed, "The intention is well-meant, but such lamentations don't suit the occasion."

"Why not?" asked another comrade. "We love fado. Those sentiments give us pleasure and emotion at the same time."

The young people applauded too, and spontaneously joined the show. They sang in chorus, maybe not in tune so much, but with great spirit. They sang the songs of the April Revolution: "Grândola, Dark City," "*Avante, Camarada*"—"forward, comrade, forward, join your voice to ours"—"The Seagull," and "*Força, Força*": "Valor, valor, we shall be the ramparts of steel."

It was nothing less than a delirium of clapping and shouts of "Long live!" as many of the participants joined in on the songs.

The joyful musical expression reflecting the collective victory did not stop there. An unexpected visitor appeared with a harmonium as night began to deepen and without asking permission started playing as an almost giddy bonus. For the first time at the Party Center there was dancing!

"It's not very proper," Joaquina mumbled. "But what can you do?"

Of the leaders, only Gabriel danced. But with him dancing were Nelo, Berta, Mila, and with great excitement, Glória, Rosário and some of their garment co-workers, and Paulo with a friend from Metalex.

Lídice, who frequented the Center regularly, wasn't there. She may have been celebrating the victory with the propaganda people she worked with. Or possibly so she wouldn't want to see her former partner David, sitting incapacitated, but contentedly tranquil.

Middle-aged men and women also took to the dance floor—some of them almost as if wanting to show off how in their day they really knew how to dance. It was fun to see them do the fancy steps from their youth, movements that didn't exactly correspond with the tunes the harmonium was playing, but still matched the rhythm of the music.

The musician paused from time to time, and everyone talked together and boasted of their success.

Rudolfo also tried to dance, but he was so big and awkward that the women eventually refused to dance with him.

Naturally, the ones who really moved were the youth. Nelo danced from beginning to end, with various girls, with Berta and Mila. As Mila was a great dancer herself, he danced more times with her. But Berta didn't like that. She went and stood right in front of them as they danced and hurled out aggressively, "Listen to me, boy! Are you going with her now?"

Everyone was there, everyone participating in the festivities. One of the women said to another of her comrades, "I would love to dance with David. He's such a lovely man. It's a shame to see him sitting there, unable to move."

Isa stayed by the door, refusing to dance with anyone who asked her.

"Nelo," Mila implored. "Go over to her. She knows you well, she won't say no to you."

Nelo went. The dancing continued.

In one of the short intervals, he rejoined Mila and Berta.

"So?" Mila asked.

"Nothing doing, *amiga*."

Berta, typically, put her own interpretation on it. "The one she'd like to be dancing with is Luís. But Luís, our brave karate kid, doesn't have the courage to ask her."

"Another of your inventions!" Nelo responded.

"You're the ones with your eyes shut. Just look at one and then the other."

"Ridiculous," Nelo said.

"The worst of it, my friends, is if the two of them go on like that, they'll never come face to face."

Exiting his office, Marco appeared at the door with no particular expression on his face and stood watching the dancing.

And at that moment, everyone saw something they never imagined possible. Isa, who had up to then stood apart watching the dance along with the older folks, who several times had refused invitations by Nelo and the other boys, Isa, whom no one had ever seen kissing anyone, crossed the room at a run, approached Marco, gave him a quick kiss, and returned into the older crowd to continue watching. Marco was the only one to understand the bravery and significance of that kiss.

And when someone later reminded him of that scene, he said he had never in his life received a kiss that so moved him, and so inspired him in his political life to take the human aspects of each individual into account.

The next day Joaquina arrived at the Party Center a little late, and shortly afterward Isa showed up to help.

"Look at the pigsty they left this place," said Joaquina indignantly. "Papers, bottles, empty cartons. Unimaginable! Well, let's get to it, dear."

If people could only see them! Brooms, dustpans, pails, wash-cloths, detergents, all in a flurry of action—much more work than ever before. But in the end, what pride they took in a job well done—the Center all washed up and shiny again, smelling fresh and clean.

Chapter 19

Moved by the fact that Rita had also taken part in the blockade, Gabriel went to Grandmother's house. Rita was home.

Remembering the trip he had made to the Algarve and her response, "I'm staying!" Gabriel timidly asked, "Want to take a drive with me?"

"Where?"

"You choose," he answered.

Rita thought a bit. "To Guincho Beach, at sunset. Okay?" And she explained her choice: When the weather is very clear, like today, sometimes exactly when the sun sets on the horizon, the light reflects across the water and at that moment you see the green streak."

"Agreed," Gabriel accepted. He also liked that beach on the Estoril coast not far from Cascais. "Let's go see the green streak."

He borrowed the car from that same amusing comrade who had loaned it to him when he went to find Rita in the Algarve. Funny guy that he was, he didn't neglect to tell Gabriel a joke. But since Gabriel didn't find it funny, the comrade let out a hilarious guffaw rich enough for two.

They arrived on time. They sat side by side on the slope of a dune forming the long, precise semicircle of the beach. From the ocean, skimming the waves that broke into foam and the sound of rumbling waters, came a fresh breeze smelling of algae and salt. As the sun was sinking, from north to south a neat horizontal line defined the meeting place between the silver sea and the roseate sky.

Captured by nature's enchantment, they kept silent for several moments.

"Will we see the green streak today?" Gabriel asked at last.

"Let's wait and see, father," Rita replied.

Through the sinuous pantomime of the clouds, the sun slowly crept down from the sky.

"We're going to have a red sunset, father."

Gabriel fixed his eyes on the horizon.

"Don't look at the ocean. father. Look beyond, look up, to the dome of the sky. That's where the first red of the clouds will appear.

And from there it will spread all the way down to the horizon when the sun finally disappears."

They remained silent again, contemplating the glorious spectacle of time and place.

"It's good being here with you, daughter." He said it out of the blue almost as if to himself.

Behind them, the majestic dark green mountains contrasted with the changing, fairylike, rose-colored firmament.

The perpetual motion of the white line of the breaking waves across the vast length of the beach sent them the unique song of the sea over the cool whiff of twilight.

"Look! Look, now!" Rita said, pointing to the sky atop the mountains. Suddenly, cloud by cloud, one even more than the next, they glowed a bright red. For a few brief instants the red belt widened, and from up high it strode down to the ocean. The red started fading in the zones it left behind and lit up those areas still reached by the sun. The whole celestial dome now showed off a magnificent variety and intensity of light surrounding the sun that, moving ever so perceptibly, was quickly vanishing from sight.

"Father, look now! See? See?"

Waiting for the sun to reach the horizon line, the sky swiftly turned the color of fire, reflecting on the sea's mirrored surface, piercing through the capricious maneuvers of the veils of clouds. In visible movement now, lowering more and more rapidly, with just a thin stripe of fire showing but shrinking fast, the sun disappeared.

For several minutes the two sat wordlessly, blissfully possessed by wonderment. reveling in the spectacle and the fresh salty air.

"Did you see?" Rita asked.

"Yes, I saw," Gabriel confirmed.

They both laughed, the two of them smiling in the knowledge of what had not happened.

They stayed there, wrapped in the singing of the waves, watching as all the color dissolved from the sky into the soft clarity of the opaque night. What the scenery lacked in light gained with the rhythmic chanting of the waves and the taste of the tossing seas carried along on the wind.

A short biographical note on the author

Manuel Tiago

MANUEL TIAGO was the pen name of Álvaro Cunhal. Edições Avante! in Lisbon, has published nine titles by Manuel Tiago: *Até amanhã, camaradas* (Until Tomorrow, Comrades), which was adapted as a Portuguese television series in 2005; *A estrela de seis pontas* (The Six-Pointed Star); *A Casa de Eulália* (The House of Eulália); *Fronteiras* (Border Crossings); *Um risco na areia* (A Line in the Sand); *Os corrécios e outros contos* (The Slackers and Other Stories); *Sala 3 e outros contos* (The 3rd Floor and Other Stories); and *Lutas e vidas* (Struggle and Life). *Cinco dias, cinco noites* (Five Days, Five Nights), adapted to film in 1996, was the first of his works of fiction to appear in English. In its continuing series of Manual Tiago books, International Publishers has so far released *Five Days, Five Nights*, *The Six-Pointed Star*, *The 3rd Floor and Other Stories of the Portuguese Resistance*, *Border Crossings*, *The Slackers*, *Eulalia's House*, and now, *A Line in the Sand*.

Álvaro Cunhal was born in Coimbra, Portugal, on November 9, 1913. He began his revolutionary activity as a student at the law school (Faculdade de Direito) of Lisbon. He participated in the student movement and was elected in 1934 as the student representative to the University Senate. He was a militant in the Federation of Portuguese Communist Youth (Federação da Juventude Comunista Portuguesa), and was elected its secretary-general in 1935. In that year he went underground and participated in Moscow in the Sixth International Communist Youth Congress. He joined the Portuguese Communist Party (Partido Comunista Português, PCP) in 1931.

Arrested in 1937 and 1940, and subjected to torture, he returned to political struggle as soon as he was freed after several months in prison. He participated in the reorganization of the PCP in the early 1940s. Again living clandestinely, he was a member of the party Secretariat from 1942 to 1949.

Arrested anew in 1949 and brought before a fascist court, he delivered a ringing denunciation of the fascist dictatorship and a defense of his party's program. Judged guilty, he remained for 11 years in fascist prisons, almost eight of them in complete isolation. On January 3, 1960, he escaped from the prison fortress at Peniche together with a group of brave communist militants. Once again called to the Secretariat of the Central Committee, he was elected Secretary General of the PCP in 1961.

Living abroad, in Moscow and Paris, from that time forward he participated in numerous congresses and gatherings with communist parties and other revolutionary forces in international conferences. He played a critical role in organizing worldwide support, especially within the socialist countries, for the independence movements in the far-flung Portuguese colonies in Africa.

After the downfall of the fascist dictatorship on April 25, 1974, he served as Minister without Portfolio in the first four provisional governments, and was elected as a deputy to the Constituent Assembly in 1975 and to the Assembly for the Republic in 1975, 1979, 1980, 1983, 1985 and 1987. He was a member of the Council of State from 1982 to 1992.

In accordance with the decisions made at the 14th Congress of the PCP in 1992 concerning renewal and a new structure of leadership, he stepped down as Secretary General of the PCP and was elected by the Central Committee as President of the National Council of the party.

In December 1996, the 15th Congress of the PCP eliminated the National Council of the party and its presidency. Cunhal was re-elected as a member of the Central Committee.

He was re-elected to the Central Committee at the 16th and 17th party congresses in December 2000 and November 2004 respectively.

Under his own name Cunhal published several books about politics. He was a gifted artist as well: A book of his collected drawings has appeared. In addition, he published an original translation of Shakespeare's *King Lear*.

He died at the age of 91 on June 13, 2005. His funeral in Lisbon was attended by half a million people. He had one daughter, Ana Cunhal. The Portuguese government issued a postage stamp in his memory and later, in 2021, another stamp commemorating the centennial of the PCP to which he had devoted his life.

About the Translator

Eric A. Gordon, a Los Angeles resident since 1990, is a native of New Haven, Connecticut. His undergraduate degree is from Yale University, where he majored in Latin American Studies. He studied Spanish five years and Portuguese two years. He also took a summer residency in Portuguese at New York University. He went on to Tulane University, where he continued studying Portuguese and wrote a master's thesis on the opera in Rio de Janeiro in the 19th century, using original sources uncovered in the Arquivo Nacional. He earned a doctorate in history, also from Tulane, writing his dissertation about the anarchist movement in Brazil in the pre-World War I era. He also studied Portuguese language and culture under a Gulbenkian Foundation fellowship in Lisbon.

International Publishers initiated its Manuel Tiago series in 2020 with Gordon's translation of *Five Days, Five Nights*, followed by *The Six-Pointed Star*. When complete, the series will comprise all nine works of fiction by Álvaro Cunhal, each appearing for the first time in English.

Gordon is the author of *Mark the Music: The Life and Work of Marc Blitzstein*, and co-author of *Ballad of an American: The Autobiography of Earl Robinson*. A memoir in short story form that he translated from Portuguese, *Waving to the Train and Other Stories*, by Hadasa Cytrynowicz, appeared in 2013 from Blue Thread Press. In 2015 he executive produced the compact disk *City of the Future: Yiddish Songs from the Former Soviet Union*, a collection of songs composed in 1931 by Samuel Polonski to the lyrics of major Soviet Yiddish poets. He is the author of a currently unpublished political autobiography.

From 1995 to 2010, Gordon was Director of the Workers Circle/ Arbeter Ring in Southern California. He previously worked at Social and Public Art Resource Center, helping to produce murals all around the city of Los Angeles, which gave him the experience to commission a mural at the Workers Circle building. He was Southern California Chapter Chair of the National Writers Union (Local 1981 UAW/AFL-CIO) for two terms. He has written for dozens of local, national, and international publications, mostly about art, music, culture, and politics. From 2014 onward, he has been a staff writer and editor for *People's World* online newspaper.

From 2006-09 Gordon took coursework toward certification as a Secular Jewish Leader, referred to in Yiddish as a *vegvayzer*. Upon graduation, he became a legal officiant certified to conduct weddings and other ceremonial functions, a role equivalent in law to a minister, priest, or rabbi. He has a similar endorsement as a Humanist celebrant for people of any background. For five years he served as a Deputy Commissioner of Civil Marriage for the County of Los Angeles, where he conducted 1500 marriages.

Eric Gordon can be contacted at ericarthurgo@gmail.com.

We briefly hear accounts of the brutal and increasingly unwinnable colonial wars in Africa. It was largely the lower-level officers (captains or lower) who finally recognized that these expensive wars were exhausting Portugal. They comprised the operational side of the overthrow of the fascist dictatorship in 1974. Are there any other historical instances you can think of where the military felled a dictatorship and introduced democracy?

Readers are reminded again and again that the popular response to the coup attempt would be unarmed and at least in this novel there appear to have been no violations of that principle. Why is this such an important point?

The President, General Spínola, is constantly calling upon the "silent majority" to turn out for the coup that will rid the country of communism and "anarchy." U.S. President Richard M. Nixon used this term—"the great silent majority"—in a speech on November 3, 1969, appealing to this supposedly broad sector of the American people to counteract the movement against the Vietnam War which had already turned public opinion. The use of this term by the planners of the coup is intentional (even without credit to Nixon). What is the moral and emotional significance of this term?

Do you remember which character in the book drew "a line in the sand" and when? Why did the author choose that character to make the title declaration?

Why do you think José decided to return to Lisbon with Gabriel? And at the end of the book, what caused Rita and Janeto to return home from the Algarve? Why did they abandon their adolescent sense of alienation from the world and join the opposition to the coup?

The author writes, "Events like these go down in history like legends. But what is a legend if not a fantasy version of the truth?" How much truth and how much legend is there in this novel? Does it matter?

Now that you have read *A Line in the Sand*, are you curious to know more about the 1974 April Revolution, the followup attempts to destroy it, and the popular resistance?

There are several examples of what might be termed "grace" in the book—Marco and Cremilde taking Gabriel in after his release from prison, Isa not reporting Rudolfo's sexual transgression, Marco's humane handling of Isa, Gabriel's patience and forbearing toward his daughter, the comrade's unquestioning loan of his car to Gabriel, Cremilde's selfless caring for her invalid relatives, the forgiveness of the volunteer who had betrayed his comrades under torture. How might you have responded in such circumstances?

On the other hand, there's also Lídice's abandonment of David after his accident, even though she clearly still loved him. How do you account for that?

The book ends with another "line in the sand"—the horizon line at Guincho Beach. Was this a fortuitous accident or a conscious literary "rhyme?" How can you compare the two "lines in the sand" that are both so critical to the meaning of the novel?

The last chapter of the book is almost entirely set in nature. The red sky is an obvious political symbol, but why does the author end with such a scene? And do you recall a previous instance in the novel of a reddish glow in the sky? Perhaps you could contrast these two scenes.

Forthcoming from International Publishers:
The final book in the complete fiction of
Manuel Tiago

UNTIL TOMORROW, COMRADES

(Até amanhã, camaradas)

Chapter 1

Sudden bursts of wind blew in from the South. With a clatter, a zinc plate coming from who knows where flew from one side of the road, made four grotesque pirouettes and curled up, silent and sad, in the gutter on the other side. Then a downpour swept the road. The men, already drenched by the drizzle that had been falling since dawn, sought shelter next to the slender trunks of the pine trees. Only two young boys were left crushing rocks, laughing at the men fleeing the rain. Cringing under the trees and pressed against them, the men shouted for them to take cover. Seeing themselves observed, the boys laughed some more, and one of them, still breaking up rocks, started sticking his long, gangling neck up high, showing the whites of his eyes and licking up the water running down his face. The other, blinking his eyes, looked at his friend, looked at the men and seemed to be saying, *We're funny, aren't we?*

"Look at those devils," said an old man, trying to wrap himself in a coat so small it seemed like a child's.

The thin little man to whom that was directed shrugged his shoulders. "The weather's not going to change today," he said with a soft, tired voice.

As if to give him confirmation, the wind blew even stronger, the air darkened, the sky reached the ground, the streams of water continued to swell. One by one, the men then left their weak covers. Some walking with determination, others in a quick run, and still others at a natural pace, as if they considered it undignified to be in a rush for such a little thing, they headed toward an isolated house a hundred or so meters away that seemed to be crouching under the rain. It was a tavern, and if not everyone was inclined to drink, at least they would have a roof overhead.

Seeing their friends going away, the two boys threw their sledgehammers to the ground. The one with the long neck flew off like an arrow, striking the puddles of water with his naked feet and waving his arms in big, disjointed gestures, possibly signaling that he was a great swimmer. The other followed, shaking with laughter. They got to the tavern before the others, but the comic, unable to wait there, went out into the rain calling the men with his arms, thereby claiming the privilege of discovering such a magnificent shelter.

They gathered in the small, dark saloon. Piled up at the door, they looked outside, intimating to the barkeeper that they were there only for a moment to protect themselves from the rain. Customers for his business were rare for the barkeeper, who quickly set to washing his already washed glasses, watching the men as if apologizing for the delay in serving them. Whether out of shame for refusing such a clear invitation, or because it seemed they couldn't just stay inside without spending a *tostão*, or by the power of vice, three men with solemn expressions went forward for drinks. Then all the others felt at ease to settle in as they pleased, some sitting around the table, some stepping away from the portal, where the rain hammered away driven by the wind.

"The weather won't change," the thin man repeated.

"It was necessary, it was necessary," said the old man, who had not yet succeeded, and never would, in fitting the tiny coat around his shoulders.

All of those men were more peasants than workers. Some even had their own little plots of land and, since the dry spell had been so long, they felt tempted to forgive the soaking and the loss of an afternoon's work. Silent and drenched, they gazed through the open rectangle of the door onto the curtain of water that almost hid the other side of the road from view, harkening to the copious, deafening sound falling away in the depths of the pine forest, attesting to the weight of the rainstorm. Even the boys kept themselves quiet, and the funny one, with a sad face that would have seemed impossible just minutes before, was trying hard to contain the tremors of cold now turning his limbs purple.

At a moment when the rain was coming down hardest, a shadow rapidly passed across the doorway and, before anyone had seen who it was, the shadow appeared again and a man entered. He was curved forward, shaking his arms and head to jiggle off the water from his coat sleeves and cap. When he had completed his operation, he straightened up and, saying hello to everyone, presented his long, angular face, with pale skin and a severe expression, his eyes standing out with their fixed gaze.

One of the boys, noticing the pants tucked into the socks, came to the door, looked out, said something to one of the men, who said to the unknown man, "Put your bike inside. There's plenty of room."

The unknown man appeared not to hear. He wiped his face and neck with a kerchief.

"Can any of you men tell me the way to Vale da Égua?" he asked.

The men looked at one another, some showing a barely disguised smile.

"To where?" a voice from the corner asked.

"Vale da Égua."

There was a brief silence, and again the men looked at one another.

"Nah, that's not around here," said another voice from the table.

"What did he say?"

"Vale da Égua."

He was definitely off-course, the old man with the little jacket informed him. He had been born there and had always lived in that place. He'd never heard of it. He was certainly off-course. The old man spoke and some smiled.

"This isn't the road to V—?" the unknown man asked.

"Yes, it is," one of the men responded. "Vvv…is just ahead. If it wasn't for so much rain, you could see the houses from here."

The stranger went to the door, looked out on the road, took off his cap and twisted it, coming back inside and slapping it on one of his hands, revealing his hair stuck to his head.

"So none of you men knows?"

"The road to where?" the barkeeper asked from the back of the room. He had heard perfectly well, but thought he should call the stranger's attention to the establishment he found himself in.

"Vale da Égua," one of the boys said.

The barkeeper stuck out his lower lip, which could have signaled that he didn't know of such a place as much as his displeasure because the stranger hadn't decided to buy anything.

"All right then, thank you!" said the unknown man. And adjusting his cap, pulling up the collar on his coat, he went to the door, looked at the sky, and headed out once again into the rain.